Ermingild

The Realm and the
Silent Rose

Ermingild

The Realm and the Silent Rose

A Fairytale for the Forgotten

CH FLINT

E

ERMINGILD
PUBLISHING

For information contact:
colleenflint@ymail.com • Ermingild.com

Published by:
Ermingild Publishing

Cover design artwork by SusansArt@99D
Interior book design by Francine Platt, Eden Graphics, Inc.
Illustrations by SusansArt@99D

Hardback ISBN 979-8-89454-131-0
Paperback ISBN 979-8-89454-130-3
eBook ISBN 979-8-89454-132-7
Audiobook ISBN 979-8-89454-133-4

Library of Congress Number: 2026909324

Manufactured in the United States of America

First Edition

To my friend, Taavi.

I'll see you in the Realm.

Léo made the walk from the outer village of Mateo towards the town of Neesa with his tiny son riding on his shoulders, dressed in the miniature blue silk caftan and cap his mother, Tashi, had made, the one that made his blue eyes even more vivid against his olive skin and curly dark hair. Tashi walked just a few steps ahead of them on the worn dirt road, she and Léo conversing sparingly as their feelings were close to the surface, but they played with Taavi to keep him happy.

Taavi now held onto handfuls of his father's hair with one hand and joyfully pounded his father's head with the other, obliging Tashi to carry her husband's cap, and then Taavi's as well, as Neesa came into view.

Today, Taavi was to enter the Realm.

The Realm was vast, surrounded by ageless stone walls that ran deep through the forests and far into the mountains, its borders more expansive than anyone knew. Its walls were formidable, and covered in deep layers of thick, woody vines, mostly brown, dead, and intertwined with a variety of protective thorny species, also dead. The gates were beautiful, but covered in old, shriveled ivy and climbing roses long past their bloom.

The small family, at last approaching the ancient gates, could see glimpses of the heavy, ornate iron with brass work overlays of animals, flowers, children, and bits of ancient text peeking through the dry vegetation. Everything on the gates had the patina of time layered over them like a hardened mist that had been gradually settling for unknown centuries, and there was an air of permanence about their decay that no one questioned.

Two bells hung in the heavily adorned iron framework arching above the double gates. A small bell with a deep red tapestry pull and a full gold tassel hung down within hand's reach. A much larger bell hung above the smaller bell, its deep blue pull hanging behind the gate, its end unseen by outsiders. The luxurious bell pulls seemed to be the only parts of the gates untouched by time.

Taavi pointed excitedly at the bells. Not old enough to find the words he wanted, he stretched his arm as high as it would go, as if he was sure he could touch them.

Léo playfully lifted Taavi off his shoulders, replacing both their caps. "It's time to go through the gates, Taavi."

He and Tashi each held one of his soft dimpled hands as they walked the last few steps to where the gates would open. From her pack, Tashi retrieved the customary offerings of bread and grain and placed them in a small, ceremonial bag.

Léo grasped just above the golden tassel and rang the smaller, higher pitched bell. Taavi cooed and laughed at hearing the beautifully clear *ting ting*, putting two of his tiny fingers into his mouth while listening in delight. He seemed mesmerized as he stood beside his parents, gazing up at the bells, as his mother hung the bag on a woven cord over his shoulder.

Léo said softly, "It's time, Tash."

Their hearts ached as they both lovingly knelt down to Taavi's level before having to send him through the gates alone.

Tashi had never been away from her little son before, and though she felt they had carefully prepared him for this parting, now that the moment had arrived, she suddenly felt that nothing they could have done could ever be enough. She felt a wave of anxiety she had not anticipated, and Léo could see the flush of panic on her face. He watched helplessly as her eyes searched Taavi's face for the right way to say goodbye.

She looked into Taavi's eyes and touched his forehead, then touched hers, touched his heart, then touched her own, then put her arms around herself to show a hug.

"Hug-gu," he said back, reaching to embrace her. All in a split second, she tried to take in one more smell of his head and memorize the feel of his tiny form as she felt him begin to turn away from her, his curiosity pulling him towards the sound of the massive gates opening.

Léo and Tashi were able to get a glimpse of the pale, ivory robes and sage colored sashes of the monks who were also accompanied by a large white dog as the monks called out to Taavi, "Come! Come little one! Welcome to the Realm! Come say hello to our friends!"

The monks held out their hands, and Taavi eagerly ran to put his little hand into one of theirs without even a backward glance. The red tapestry rope was pulled inside, allowing only one child at a time to enter the Realm, and the gates closed carefully behind him.

After so much preparation and anxiety, Taavi's sudden absence made his parents feel that their world was abruptly silent and empty. They simply stood outside the gates for a few minutes, unsure of what to do with themselves.

Léo at last sighed, then spoke. "I don't remember any of my time here; I was just too small."

Tashi nodded, pulling her small slate and pencil from her pack. Pointing at herself, she wrote, *Same.* She paused, looking up at the great bell on top. *How long?*

"I'd assume your guess is as good as mine," he responded, putting his arms around her reassuringly. "I think I heard once of someone's child taking three days, but that …"

She interrupted by abruptly shaking her head. *Too long,* she wrote in large letters. She erased her words quickly and wrote again. *Taavi too little!* She pointed at the gate, then to herself and Léo, *Needs us?* She looked pleadingly at Léo. They both knew all contact with the Keepers was forbidden.

"Whatever happens in there, we know we all get through it," he replied soothingly. He gently smoothed a stray curl, one of her many long, dark ringlets that cascaded down her back. "He's a good boy, and you've been the best mama to him, so he's going to be all right." He cradled her face in his hands, kissed her on her forehead, then gently leaned her head into his chest.

He partially broke their embrace as he noticed a flash of familiar fur in the cobblestone streets nearby. "… and look!" He pointed, smiling, with a hint of amusement in his voice, "Here come our friends to wait with us." He managed to get a reluctant smile out of her, even as she wiped a tear, as she saw their family's companions.

Léo's beloved Corgi, Jett, came bounding up to them, along with Tashi's little squirrel who had accompanied them on their journey. The animals had stayed far off the trails exploring, only now catching up to them. The little squirrel, Angel, held tightly to Jett's fur like a tiny stowaway. Angel, sensing Tashi's worry, ran to her, scurried up her arm, then over her shoulder, holding tightly to her bright scarf so she could cradle against her chest.

"Think of how happy Taavi will be to receive his Guardian," Léo encouraged, giving Angel a welcoming scritch on her head with his fingertips, while bending down slightly to peer into Angel's face.

Tashi nodded, sighing deeply. She stroked Angel's fur soothingly, as another tear slipped down her cheek. She had held her emotions back, staying cheerful for Taavi, but now everything was all starting to come out, the fear of being away from him for the first time, and not knowing how long it would be. No longer holding back her tears, her heart sank as she held the little squirrel, just as if it were a baby in her arms. Léo again held her close, beginning to turn her away from the gates.

Jett, sensing Léo's concern for Tashi, led them a little way past the gates where a small creek exited the Realm, a section of the wall having been built on top of some coarse rock to let the water through. The creek branched out into a lovely meadow on the edge of Neesa, near enough to the gates they would not miss hearing the ringing of the second, larger bell. The monks would ring it to signal that Taavi had indeed found his Guardian and would be allowed to come back to them.

The gentle sounds of the creek sparkling over the stones muffled the sounds of the town, giving Tashi some welcome privacy. Trees grew near the water where she now sat holding Angel, and she finally rested from the long walk. The grass was soft beneath her slippers, and the breeze delicately ruffled through the leaves that gently filtered and cooled the afternoon sunlight where Léo came to sit beside her.

The birds and animals that came here seemed to speak in a silent language to each other as they came to drink the cool, sweet water. Some lingered, looking at Léo and Tashi. A few came to gently touch noses with Jett, while clusters of birds flew into the Realm and back again, settling to rest in the nearby trees. The calming scents of the natural garden were of honeysuckle and rushing water, and the couple was soon lulled to sleep after the tiring walk and the emotions of the day, with Jett watching faithfully nearby, and Angel cuddled close in Tashi's arms.

Only the animals knew this place as Ermingild.

2

WITH TAAVI having newly entered the Realm, the monks intended to hold onto his hands to help gently lead him away from the gates and into the beautiful outer gardens.

Instead, Taavi quickly held out his arms, reaching towards a large, white goose who came stepping out in dignified fashion from around the fragrant rose hedges, several ducks waddling not far behind her. The ringing of the small bell signaled an important rite of passage for the children on the world of Placidéo. The birds always seemed to eagerly await its glad tidings as well, as a variety of colorful songbirds now left the carved stone fountains to flit to the ornate shrubbery and trees lining the rock pathway to get a closer look at the new arrival.

Kneeling down, a tall, somewhat elderly monk said to Taavi, "My name is Silas, and these are my friends, Jarek and Saren." He then extended his hand to pet the goose affectionately. "Let me introduce you to Willow. She'll be your first friend."

Taavi held his breath in excitement as the goose gently put her head over his shoulder, resting her soft neck briefly against his while breathing quiet honking sounds. Taavi hugged Willow, patting her back, softly saying, "Lillow, Lillow, I hug-gu Lillow."

Willow carefully encouraged Taavi to follow her, nibbling at his caftan ever so softly with her bill, the ducks falling in behind, as they all walked down a hill towards a lake that could be seen peeking through some small hills of bright flowers.

Old Silas and the two younger monks followed attentively, along with the big white dog who stayed quite close to Silas. He was an old Great Pyrenees dog named Zeke, short for Ezekiel.

Taavi was able to get glimpses of an idyllic scene while walking down a gradually steeper mossy path with his toddling steps. A long, winding lake now came into full view, extending far back into a deep valley with large meadows on each side which merged into pine forests. The lake was filled with fresh, clear water, fed by a large creek that tumbled from far up into the mountains. Small herds of the loveliest of animals such as sheep and ponies grazed upon the sweet, green grasses of the meadows. Forest animals were on the edges of the fields, and all was calm. An elegant red and stone barn, several stories high, had been built for any animals who desired to live there. Its massive wooden beams spanned like a bridge all the way across a narrow place on the lake, creating a picturesque reflection of itself on the still waters. Flowers grew everywhere, and their scent mixed with the fresh smell of the pine forests and the coolness of the water.

Willow and the ducks stopped a few paces before reaching the lake, eyeing Taavi's ceremonial bag with great interest. The grain offering was still inside of it, along with the bread offering his mother had so carefully baked just for today. Tashi had made the round loaf using strips of dough woven into a unique, intricate knot used by her family for generations, her very best work, with the finest flour she could acquire.

The earlier ringing of the small bell had also served as a sign for all in the Realm who wished, that it would soon be time to come and partake of the beautiful bread and fresh grain, though the partakers were perhaps not who the Placidéans imagined.

Saren sat beside Taavi and helped him open his sack. "How would you like to share what's in here with some of your new friends? Would you like to give them the grain first?"

Taavi smiled and nodded, and with Saren's help, Taavi's senses were soon filled with a lovely rush of fluttering, colorful wings and the sounds of the varied calls of many feathered species as he scattered the grain, watching the birds fly in from all directions to eat. Saren helped him hold some of the grain in his hand, and Taavi laughed as a tiny bird landed on his upturned palm to eat, brave enough to fly within the midst of so many larger fowl.

Next came the beautiful loaf of bread. Taavi couldn't help but taste it first; he knew his mother's bread would be so soft it would seem to melt in his mouth. Saren helped him break it apart into small pieces and toss it, some into the water, some onto the meadow grass, and even some into the air. How the birds rushed to eagerly get every last bit.

Almost as quickly as it all began, it was over, and when most of his feathered guests had departed, Taavi sat on the edge of the lake, feeling content, with Willow and her duck friends still beside him. Two of the ducks slipped into the now serene water, creating small, overlapping chevron ripples on the lake's surface.

Willow settled down for a nap next to Taavi, plucking bits of grass within reach to eat as she did so. A pair of kittens came and began to gently bat at the small tassels on his caftan, while Jarek brought soft, white blankets and pillows, fluffy, and thickly embroidered with images of the Realm's beauty. Deep with softness and warmth, they were scented with dried herbs and flowers from the formal gardens, and soon, a little fawn pug named Wags came to cuddle on the fresh bedding.

Silas came back with Zeke, bringing a snack of honey and hot biscuits and a cup of fresh milk.

Taavi let out a deep, contented sigh as he bit into one of the warm biscuits, sharing a taste with Wags. There was yellow butter soaked into every flaky crevice, and the honey on top melted into the butter, making him feel more full and cozy with every bite. The milk was fresh and cool, leaving moisture on the outside of the ornate tin cup that had double handles for little hands. *Daphne* was beautifully inscribed in the tin, the name of the cow who shared the milk and the butter.

When Taavi's snack was finished, the little pug set to work as only a pug could, intensely sniffing and snuffling to clean up every fallen crumb, carefully cleaning up Taavi as well, before once again settling amongst all the pillows and blankets.

More animals began to visit, much to Taavi's delight.

Because Taavi would not find his Guardian; Taavi's Guardian would find him.

This was the Realm.

EARLIER THAT SAME DAY on a lonely and little-known farm between Mateo and Neesa, a baby was born to Zant and Mirran. They had no Guardians in their home. Whether they were too depressed to care for them, or had hearts too dark for their Guardian companions to remain was not known except to them.

The night before, when the pains started, Mirran's mother, Savta, came to help with the birth, bringing her little fawn pug with her named Rowdy.

Savta ached inside as she looked around the home, not untidy, but with no signs anywhere that a child was coming. She needed supplies if she was going to deliver this baby, and she set about first thing to find what she would need.

There were no baby blankets.

Looking around, she found some clean towels she would need for the birth, and she could also use some of them for bedding and blankets to wrap the baby when it was born, though they wouldn't be nearly as soft as she would prefer to welcome a newborn.

No baby clothes.

She rummaged deeper into some lower cupboards. She found some spare linens she quickly tore and folded into diapers and some makeshift wraps. There wasn't time to sew a single stitch; these would have to do.

Her heart hurt and her stomach was sick. She never could understand what had happened to her daughter. To this couple. She remembered Mirran's Guardian, the beautiful black bunny named Nyx, and how she worried when Mirran's fiancé had no Guardian when they were courting.

But there was no time for thinking of that now. Her concern was this baby. She pushed on.

No cradle.

She began searching again, and finally, in the dark of the barn by lantern light, she found an old, wooden toolbox. It was filthy, covered in spider webs, dirt, and old straw.

In the moonlight, she dragged it to the well, and with nothing but an old rag and some nearby sand, she rolled up the sleeves of her dress and prepared to clean. She pulled the well handle up and down, and as she brought the water from the depths of Placidéo, she brought grief and conflict from the depths of her soul, her tears falling with the water as she started scrubbing with the rag and the coarse sand.

How she longed to simply take this baby and disappear. How many times had she thought to do it? It's not like they wanted the baby at all. Just like Nyx. It was forbidden on Placidéo to ever harm a Guardian, and when Nyx appeared at her door, shivering with fright, she scooped him into her arms, determined to protect him from Zant and let Mirran think the bunny had simply vanished. She wasn't sure if Mirran would even keep herself safe from Zant if need be.

But she knew she was simply too old now, and there was no one to help her escape, let alone hide her and a baby. She could not support herself if she left her little farm, and it was not worth enough for her to live off the money if she sold it. If she tried to confront them and their cold disregard for this baby, she would surely be forbidden to come to the house.

Her thoughts tore at her heart more than the coarse sand on the skin of her fingers. She was a proud woman, a protector, strong, and the reality of this defeat stung deeply. She would be forced to play a weak, servile role to save her grandchild. But she would do whatever was necessary.

Rinsing the toolbox one last time in the fresh water, she took in deep breaths of the cool night air before lugging the box into the house, setting it by the stove to dry. Later in the night, when the wood had dried, she lined it with the improvised blankets she had made up.

Mirran required all her attention now, and a baby girl was born just as the sun rose. She had tiny golden curls and newborn baby blue eyes, just the color of the sky at sunrise. She never cried, and her parents simply called her, *The Child.*

"Do you want any other name for her?" Savta

asked carefully as she wrapped the newborn in some of the fabrics she had found.

"She's just The Child; that's what she is," Mirran answered shortly, exhausted from laboring and relieved to finally be done.

Renewing her resolve, Savta summoned all her inner strength and pushed down her emotions. She laid the baby down in the toolbox. Rowdy, sensing Savta's love and worry for this tiny human, laid down as close as possible to the baby while Savta tended to all that needed to be done.

Finishing her work, she picked up the child one more time, holding the soft little bundle to her face while her mother now slept, and her father went outside without saying a word, flask in his vest.

"I love you, Little One," she whispered. "Don't worry, Grandma will be close by … always." She slowly swayed as long as she dared, taking in her sweet newborn smell, and humming an ancient melody. Her heart grieved inside, knowing it was time to go, and she cuddled her cheek on the baby's soft skin. Reluctantly settling her back down in the toolbox, she turned to leave.

"Come, Rowdy," she said in a whisper, and the little pug, usually playful and reluctant to obey, followed quickly by her feet.

After her short walk home, Savta checked on her sheep, let Little Cow and her baby out to pasture from the small red barn, and went inside her cottage. She fed Rowdy a late breakfast and found the scrap end of a loaf of bread to eat for herself. She didn't feel like sleeping, and immediately she began to sew for the baby.

She felt better when her hands were busy.

She would make her little pink dresses in all different sizes for when she grew bigger, and little pairs of pink shoes with knitted stockings for when she would learn to walk. She would make her a little pink bag with a strap to match her little outfits, and she would make a beautiful dusty-pink cloak with a hood, with pink silk ribbon ties that would tie beneath her chin on one side with a bow.

Pink, the color of the climbing roses that grew thickly over her tiny stone cottage all year round, the cottage with the arched wooden door, surrounded by the stick fence that let Rowdy play outside, and kept the sheep out of her flower gardens, the little cottage surrounded by rolling green sheep meadows fading into pine forests. Pink, the color of the curtains in her kitchen where spring water fed through an opening in the wall, running through a trough in her work board, then out the other side and down a little rock path into the pond for the animals, right next to the red barn, all day and night, making a pleasant trickling sound just outside the house.

To The Child, in her very early years, this place would grow to be loved in her heart as the most beautiful on Placidéo.

ON A MOSSY PLACE where the meadow met the edge of the pine forest, a porcupine could be seen. The day was coming to an end in the Realm, and he didn't look to be in a hurry as he began to slowly amble his way down the hill in the direction of the lake.

Saren noticed him first. "Look there," he said to Jarek and Silas. "Is that Quill?"

"Yes," said Silas, stroking his beard with one hand, and patting Zeke with the other. "Curious, though. He's not been here for a long, long time. We should inform Gideon and Petra."

Zeke wagged slowly and let out a bark as he recognized Quill in the distance.

Upon receiving word that Quill had arrived,

Gideon and Petra, two of the oldest Keepers, decided to spend the evening by the lake with the others, and watch the moonrise. They kept a casual eye on Quill along with the other Guardians while enjoying a rest from the day's work.

Sunset was a favorite time in the Realm and tonight did not disappoint as the sun began sending vivid late colors across the sky. Placidéo almost always had full moonlight, but the Realm also had its own distinctive light at sunset.

Except for the pine trees which formed a protective canopy over the mountains, all leafy plants and grasses gave off a unique form of light when darkness fell, giving even the most unassuming plants the look of stained glass as if sunlight was shining through them. This caused there to be no shadow on any surface of the plants, top or bottom. Stems and leaves were every hue of green and served to enhance the intense colors of the flowers. Each blossom became an exquisite work of glowing color. Rich, veined purples, reds, and blues, warm yellows, oranges, and coppers, all shone with indescribable beauty. Looking at them was like gazing at the stained glass windows of the most magnificent cathedral one could imagine.

And in a very real sense, the ethereal light made it feel sacred like the cathedral it was, as at night, the spirits of the Guardians who had been before, and were yet to be, could visit as they wished, to mingle with the Guardians present amid the prisms of rich color.

Taavi watched families of small rabbits, squirrels, and other animals as they leaped together in joyful reunion. At a distance, he could see groups of dogs, horses, and even great herds of exotic animals, running full speed in play through the meadows nearby. What was beautiful in daylight, at night, was breathtaking in this pure form of light.

Quill, after observing everything from a distance, finally came to see Taavi, who looked wide eyed at the porcupine. Knowing that most children eagerly loved to touch all the animals, Quill stayed back just a bit, aware of his physical uniqueness.

Petra looked on while Jarek said, "Taavi, this is Quill. Would you like to pet him?"

Taavi was beginning to get sleepy, but he smiled and nodded.

"Let me hold your hand, and we'll do it together, all right?"

Taavi held out his hand, and Quill stepped up to him, looking into his eyes thoughtfully. Jarek gently brushed Taavi's hand down Quill's back, then softly around Quill's face as Taavi stared back, smiling. "I pet Quill." Then Taavi's voice grew soft, "Nice Quill."

Quill put his front paws up on Taavi's lap, looking even more deeply into his eyes for a moment longer before turning to sit down near Willow. Several nearby birds quickly flew off in different directions after listening to what Quill had to say to her, followed by other birds dispersing into further parts of the meadows. As they did so, a hush traveled up the valley. Wags let out a deep, noisy sigh before settling back to sleep, and was soon joined by Taavi, who finally laid down on the pillows and closed his eyes for the night.

A while later, Silas returned from nearby where he had been resting by the lake shore with Zeke, followed by Saren, who said, "The Guardians just became rather uneasy. Do you know what's happening?"

Gideon nodded and said, "Agreed." Then he asked Petra in a somewhat curious tone, "Is Quill to be Taavi's Guardian?"

"No," she hushed in a serious tone, looking over at Jarek who nodded. She continued, "Quill says the Emissaries have sensed a grave circumstance and are gathering from far throughout the deep forests. They are traveling here now, desiring to meet with the Guardians. He says Taavi is the one, and he is to stay until they arrive, and no Guardian is to be chosen before that time." She began to turn. "I must do a Realm's Proclamation. Follow me."

Petra, an ancient one and of slight stature, made her way further up the shore of the lake to an old, heavily carved stone gazebo hidden by some trees. A stone box built into it held many ancient artifacts of the Realm, including The Keeper's Robe and Sash of the Seven Emissaries which was placed upon her by three of the monks, over the top of her ivory robe and sage sash. The heavy, sage green robe with its dark blue sash dwarfed her tiny frame, but she stood firm beneath the weight of its heavy gold embroidery, doing her best to rise to a dignified posture.

All the nearby Keepers stopped what they were doing and gave her their full attention. The moonlight from one of Placidéo's three moons shone off the robe's richly stitched forest motif accompanied by hundreds of lines of ancient text of the Realm, as well as Petra's polished white hair, smoothed back into a small knot as she held her arms out in preparation for the formal announcement.

Looking up at the sky, she proclaimed simply, "Let it be known to all in the Realm: The Emissaries are coming." Then bowing her head, and lowering her arms, she finished, "Let us prepare."

Two monks then removed a long, ornately carved, stone staff that was suspended from two ornate corbels at head's height across the center of the gazebo, while two more helped Petra remove the Keeper's Robe. The staff was threaded through the sleeves of the robe which would now be hung in the gazebo and displayed along with the sash for as long as the Emissaries remained.

Petra now extended her arms towards the sky facing the lake as the monks prepared to replace the ends of the staff back into their decorative corbels. As they locked into place, the sound of it seemed to resonate against the stone, followed by a moment of silence.

Petra dropped her arms suddenly, and immediately, an elegant, red-crowned crane emerged from under the still waters next to the shore. As it broke the surface of the lake, the sound echoed inside the stone structure. The snow-white bird took flight, water shimmering in the moonlight as it fell in sheets from his rising wings before his white form became silhouetted against the dark night sky, disappearing as it flew up the lake towards the mountains.

And for just a moment, the entire Realm seemed to hold its breath.

5

SILVER SAFEERAH LILIES had sprung up in the night at the edge of the forest in anticipation of the arrival of the Emissaries, creating a natural floral carpet where the meeting was to take place. Legend said she was but a single plant, present at the very creation of Placidéo, and her roots spread far throughout the upper meadow. She could lay dormant under the Realm's soil indefinitely until she felt a need to be present, at which time the lilies never failed to grow nearly instantaneously, blooming into intricate, organized patterns of her choice, close to the ground, far across the expanse of the bright green grasses of the Realm.

Safeerah lilies were sensitive, intelligent, and highly cherished by all, and the Keepers took tender care that her ground was never disturbed. The sentient blossoms were known to express deep layers of knowledge of the Realm, however, the ability to interpret the feelings of the Safeerah lilies was a skilled and ancient art, only partially known by just a few of the most senior monks. Safeerah was highly selective of her audience and what she chose to share.

With the proclamation ceremony now complete, Petra was informed of the appearance of the lilies. Satisfied, she quietly stepped down to the edge of the lake and waited for her helpers to join her. "We all must be ready by dawn," she began. "Silas, Gideon, you'll be with me at the meeting of the Emissaries. We must stay in seclusion until just before it begins. Jarek and Saren, you'll stay with Taavi. Let's see what this day reveals. Oh, and also, a watch must be assigned at the gazebo."

Back at the gazebo, seven lanterns had been hung between the seven supporting stone pillars of its structure, and now, the monk assigned to keep watch of the skies above the lake had seen the sign; a constellation of seven stars had moved into orbit straight above them. She now lit each lantern, the beautiful lights shining against the lake waters, the gentle signal that all was well, and all parties may proceed when ready.

The hour just before sunrise was filled with great anticipation as both the Guardians and monks officially gathered to await the arrival of the Seven Emissaries from the forest.

At dawn, they appeared as expected, quietly stepping just into the distant edge of the meadow, carefully placing their footfalls between the exquisite lilies, a grand delegation from deep in the mountains of the Realm.

There were two great bears, one brown and one white, along with a moose and an elk, both with large racks of antlers. An eagle folded in his large wings after gliding to an elegant landing on a nearby rock. A pair of white horses tossed their heads in regal fashion, walking into the meadow to complete the council. The lilies had formed proper places for each Emissary, the three monks, and Zeke, and had also created beautifully bordered areas for the Guardians to gather.

Only the monks possessed the gift to interpret the mostly silent communication between the Guardians, so the three of them gathered quietly, sitting on the cool grass as the lilies had directed, each having meditated in solitude to prepare for this rare and important occasion. Silas couldn't help but breathe in deeply as he noted the mild, sweet fragrance of the lilies all around them. As he took his seat amongst them on the grass, he noted their silver petals, veining, and centers. Zeke immediately lay down next to him contentedly, and Silas acknowledged him with an affectionate pat on his head. "Good boy, Zeke. That's my good boy," he said quietly.

First to greet the mighty elk who headed the council was Quill. He confirmed he had identified Taavi and then stepped aside as the last few Guardians gathered, including Willow. The great elk pawed his front foot to begin, with three Emissary council members on either side of him as he delivered the fateful news on behalf of them all. Their regal and solemn demeanor reflected the serious nature of what was being announced. An earnest discussion then ensued amongst the

Guardians as to what was to be done.

Silas wondered if it was just his imagination, or if the scent of the lilies was not as sweet as he struggled with the nature of what he had just heard. Questioning if perhaps he was possibly interpreting incorrectly, he flashed a quick glance over at Gideon and Petra, but he could get no information on what they were feeling. He increased his concentration to be able to discern as much as he could of what was happening as there were now so many voices at once. Closing his eyes, he leaned against Zeke's sturdy frame, resting his head against his shoulder as the discussion continued, desperately hoping that what he had gleaned was wrong. Zeke could sense his distress and licked Silas's hands briefly in encouragement.

The Guardians had not come to agreement, except to recess the meeting to think on their own and meet again later, and all gradually retreated, spreading quietly throughout the meadow. Willow sadly spread her wings to drift back down the hill to Taavi, who was still asleep next to Wags.

Silas knew now there was no mistake; the scent

of the lilies was weakening. Now having time to closely examine the lilies, he felt a chill run through him as he saw that their silver petals had faint black veining extending out from the center of the blossoms. This was something he had never heard of, and though his knowledge of Safeerah lilies was limited, the veining, along with the news of the Emissaries, had his mind deeply disturbed.

Zeke whined softly, putting his paw on Silas. For now, this was all he could do. Silas absently hugged the dog, waiting for the other monks to act.

All three now sat in a combination of stunned silence, mental exhaustion, and shock. As Keepers of the Realm, they could not interfere with the procedures nor the will of the Guardians. No matter what, they were to do what was necessary to help them carry out their duties while also maintaining the sanctity and protocols of the Realm.

Now, each in their own way, was struggling to review all they had been taught about the strict limits set by this ancient order while also trying to process what had just been told by the Emissaries before trying to speak out loud.

Finally, Gideon spoke, his voice low. "Do either of you two know what this great evil is that is coming to Placidéo?"

Silas remained still, his arms locked around Zeke, and Petra just shook her head. She finally answered, but even more quietly. "I don't, and I do not believe the Emissaries do, either; they just know it is coming. It demands the life of a child, and they know that someday in the future, it will take Taavi."

Silas immediately asked, alarmed as his deepest fears were confirmed. "Is it really possible to expect that a Guardian could prevent this? And forgive me, but I have to ask, are we as Keepers truly powerless to do anything to stop this? There is no precedent. Nothing like this has ever happened on Placidéo."

Petra turned to him. "This is *precisely* the debate among the Guardians. We don't believe it has ever happened on Placidéo, and they *absolutely* want to prevent it." She met his eyes and looked at him compassionately before continuing. "I know this is shocking. I feel this disturbance deeply as well, but we must trust the Guardians." Then she continued with kind but firm resolve, "… and we must maintain our proper place in the Realm as it has existed for as long as time."

"Again," he struggled, "forgive me." And he turned away, his arm around Zeke's shoulder, petting him as he continued in deep thought, the scent of the lilies continuing to fade.

When Taavi finally woke up, he was completely unaware that his future was the topic of serious and urgent conversation between all the animals. Was there a Guardian who could save him? He was such a happy little boy. He had his breakfast which included a baked pudding served with sweet berries from the gardens, and then for the rest of the day, he explored some of the many things to see in the Realm with Willow and Wags by his side.

Throughout the Realm, the Guardians talked amongst themselves while the Emissaries waited patiently for them to decide what they could do to help Taavi.

Day two ended with no answers, and day three began with Gideon, Petra, Silas, and Zeke continuing their watch over the many Guardians coming and going to meet with each other at the edge of the forest where the Great Council of Emissaries presided.

At last, a final meeting of the Guardians was called by the Emissaries. A decision simply must be made, and there was nothing more to be said even though some of the Guardians wanted to know if there was any new information that could help them. There was none.

Amidst this backdrop of hopeless impasse, Petra interpreted for the elk. "We need to stay together and decide what we are going to do, and we will not break again until we have found a way forward. Taavi cannot stay here indefinitely; he must be returned to his parents. Unfortunately, if this dark prediction is not overcome, the child's fate seems certain. If no one feels called to accept Guardianship, then it will sadly be the decision of the Emissaries to send this child forth alone to face the fulfilment of this evil prophecy, but we will only do this with full consensus."

Everything fell quiet.

For a long time, no one moved or made a sound.

At length, Silas was startled to feel Zeke stand. The ancient dog rose with calm dignity. He had his usual stiffness of old age in his movement, his white fur hiding his silver, as he approached the Emissaries.

Petra whispered Zeke's words as everything in the Realm seemed to suddenly stop and go even more silent than it already was.

"I will be Taavi's Guardian."

The lilies instantly turned as white as fresh snowfall, and a sweet scent filled the nearby Realm.

Silas caught his breath, desperately attempting to discern for himself what was being said while he worked at keeping his own reaction in check as many of the Guardians who heard were also taken by surprise at such a suggestion. A flurry of questions and concerns quickly arose amongst them, and all three monks listened intently.

Guardians are usually assigned young. He was old. How would he be able to protect Taavi? How could he prevent this evil? No one had even figured out what it was.

Zeke did not respond but waited patiently for the flood of reactions to stop.

He stood humbly before them all, yet still so dignified … Zeke, the oldest of the Guardians who had taught so many of them, yet never left the Realm to become a Guardian himself, beloved by so many as a quiet, faithful presence for as long as anyone could remember.

Petra now interpreted softly for Zeke. "I must remind you all that it is the gift of the Guardians to foresee the future of the children who come to us as well as their needs and their personalities, and we assign the Guardian who will best help the child fulfil that future, but we don't have the power to change it, just like we can't change the world outside the Realm. That is why we're not gifted to clearly see the evil that seems destined to befall Taavi. It is veiled to us. But I am an Ancient One, and I promise to love and protect Taavi in the best way I know how. You all must trust me. Now let me go."

A new silence accompanied by a deep sadness began to settle over the Guardians and also the monks. Their love for Zeke, as well as for Taavi, and the truth of what Zeke was saying, along with their fear of the unknown for them both, was falling hard on all of them.

At last, the elk stepped forward to proclaim acceptance on behalf of the Council and all the Realm.

Gideon briefly rested one hand on Silas in a quiet show of understanding. Everyone knew of the special bond between Silas and Zeke. Despite how long Silas had loved this old dog, he knew he had to give him up if there was even a chance to save the little boy, and he was determined to properly fulfil his role as a Keeper of the Realm.

Petra excused Silas from his Emissarial duties to go be with Taavi, and he was grateful for the chance to be alone to sort his thoughts and feelings as he walked down the hill. His mind filled with memories of Zeke, his constant and faithful friend. He already felt the loneliness beginning as his hand fell to his side and Zeke wasn't there, wet nose pushing against him for pets, his tail thumping busily for whatever was planned. Zeke had been with him for so long, he somehow thought he would never leave, and he had an ache in his chest as the reality of losing his companionship was rapidly closing in on his old heart.

Well ahead of him, Willow again spread her white wings to glide down the valley, taking her place by the lake shore for the final time as Taavi's friend and his guide to the Realm, while back at the top of the meadow, one by one, the Emissaries gently rested their heads against Zeke's head to quietly pronounce their unique blessings upon him. The words they uttered were known only to Zeke, and each Emissary took careful, thoughtful time to meditate upon Zeke's mission to help Taavi, carefully passing on to him whatever wisdom they could. Zeke held up his paw respectfully to each of them in turn.

Petra spoke again for the elk. "Our Emissarial duties are now complete. We wish to say that we are pleased with the decisions made here today. We also proclaim unanimously that there could not be a finer Guardian in the history of the Realm to accept this assignment than Ezekiel. Let us all turn to show him reverence for his great courage as he accepts this unknown mission on behalf of Taavi."

All the remaining Guardians turned respectfully to watch Zeke leave the presence of the Emissaries to make the long walk down the meadow to Taavi.

Safeerah began to weep … first out of love for Zeke and his great love for Taavi, as well as her own sadness for the difficulty of their way, and her admiration for Zeke's mission, his self-sacrifice, but then there was more, and she couldn't remember what it was. She felt overwhelming emotions, sadness, grief, even great pain … the emotions belonged to something else … they came as she thought of Taavi …

From deep within Placidéo she sensed a stirring of ancient knowledge, long forgotten to her conscious thoughts. She needed to go back down within her roots, to sink back down into the rich layers of her home to rest, to think, to try to find the memories that she knew were connected to what she was feeling.

Starting from the place she had outlined with lilies for Zeke in the meadow, each blossom sprung forth tears from its center before turning from pure white to blood red in pain and disappearing back into the ground, until every bloom had done the same … vanishing … weeping beneath the Realm's soil ….

… the children … so long ago … too far back to remember … something about the children …

Silas, reaching the edge of the lake before Zeke, beckoned to Jarek and Saren to quietly let them know what had just happened. They shook their heads ever so slightly in shock to find out Zeke was leaving but were ready to help with what needed to be done, gently clapping Silas on the back in support.

As Zeke reached Taavi, the Emissaries, having waited out of respect, now turned and retreated into the forest. Just before disappearing, one of the great horses turned to Quill, arching her graceful, white neck before reaching her nose down to him.

"There will be a witness?" Gideon questioningly interpreted to Petra.

"There is always a witness to our sorrows and suffering, even if unseen," Petra confirmed. "But I do not know what this has to do with the business of the Guardians. This Emissary has foreseen this. And we can only wait to understand the fulfilment, if we ever do."

The horse then continued into the forest. As her white form faded from sight into the trees, the Keeper's Robe and Sash of the Seven Emissaries were reverently returned to the stone box in the gazebo. The lamps would remain lit until moonrise, when a torch would transfer each flame to a sky lantern. As each of the lanterns rose into the sky, the seven stars would disappear one by one, officially ending the Time of the Emissaries.

Back at the lake, Taavi looked up into Zeke's dark eyes as the great dog towered above him. Silas knelt down next to them. "Taavi, I would like you to meet your most special friend. His name is

Ezekiel." Everything was happening so fast. He felt his throat choking up and could not continue.

Saren watched his old friend stand and turn his back, overcome with emotion, tears in his own eyes as he continued for him, "…but you can call him Zeke."

Taavi stepped back, slightly nervous, pointing up at Zeke. "Big!"

Saren assured him, "It's okay, he's one of our very best friends here. You're going to love him very much."

Taavi stepped forward, reached up, and patted the huge dog carefully while whispering, "Zeke," as if trying out the name. Zeke held up a paw and wrapped it around Taavi, winning a genuine smile from the tiny boy. "He hug me."

Saren asked, "Would you like Zeke to go home with you?"

Taavi nodded up and down as big as he could and put one arm around Zeke.

Jarek had quietly walked away for a moment, and had now returned, slipping a Realm's collar into Silas's hand, lingering for a moment in a supportive hand clasp as he did, before joining Saren and Taavi.

The two younger monks knelt down, spending a few minutes helping Taavi get to know Zeke. Since they never thought the beloved old dog would leave the Realm, they took a moment and ran their hands across his broad back and rubbed his ears, telling him, "Good boy," while Zeke, sensing their anxiety and sadness, simply wagged and held out his paw for a shake. It was all he could do for them.

Silas had now composed himself and spoke gently to Taavi, "Always be a good boy and take very good care of Zeke, and then Zeke will always be with you and take good care of you, too. Let's put this special collar on him and head towards the gate, and then you can ring the bell, okay?"

"Oh, yes!" Taavi clapped, quickly returning his arms to Zeke. But he paused, looking longingly back at Willow and Wags. "Bye-bye, Lillow. Bye-bye, Wags." He walked towards them to pet them good-bye and talk to them for a few minutes. The two younger monks went with him to say his farewells, giving Silas the moment he desperately needed.

With gentle reverence, Silas placed the beautifully woven Realm's collar on Zeke, and while looking directly into his eyes, he spoke softly, "I love you, Zeke. I know you'll be a good boy and watch out for Taavi …" He now took Zeke's head in both his hands, putting his own face directly against Zeke's. "… but I need to know you'll be careful and come back home to me … somehow … none of us understand what's going to be happening out there … but promise me I'll see you again … I just really need to know this isn't goodbye."

He threw off the last tears that had escaped, gathered all his emotional strength, kissed Zeke on the head, and rose to his feet. "Time to go, Taavi," he said cheerily.

Willow and Wags followed Taavi and Zeke to the gate along with the three monks. Upon reaching the gates, Silas picked up Taavi and hugged him tight before setting him back down, playfully settling his blue silk cap on his head. He placed the blue tapestry bell pull in Taavi's hands and helped him ring the great bell. "You're a good boy, Taavi, you'll be all right." Silas couldn't help but feel like he said it to himself more than Taavi.

As the ancient gates opened, all of the sorrow and the worry born by Taavi's parents when he entered the Realm, was now multiplied and born by the monks, Silas most of all, as Taavi left the Realm.

6

Five Years Later

"Little One!"

The Child heard Grandma's voice outside. She was coming up the path bringing Rowdy with her, and The Child's heart skipped with joy. She scurried to the doorway of her home to greet her. Before she could hug Grandma, the little pug came bounding up and jumped on her, making her plop down hard on her bottom. He waggled in uncontrollable happiness, covering The Child in licks and slobbery greetings so she could hardly pet him.

"Oh, Rowdy! You know better, come back here!" Grandma laughed in surrender. Rowdy never listened.

"Here, Little One, I brought some bread I just baked." She made her way to the kitchen board and started slicing the warm loaf, filling the room with the comforting aroma.

The Child gratefully took a slice, not even waiting for butter or jam to go on top, quickly glancing to see if she could eat it before her dad noticed, in case he might take it away. She was so desperately hungry. Besides, maybe if she was good…

Grandma called, "Zant, can I take The Child home with me tonight? You know how lonely I get over at the cottage!"

"I don't care … keep her as long as you want," came her father's reply from the other room.

"Ok, thanks! I left some sliced warm bread on the kitchen board for you!"

The Child's heart felt free like a bird in flight, yet she still quietly tip-toed out of the house, taking big bites of the bread, afraid to breathe until she made it past the door and down the path. Rowdy ran around her feet excitedly. Grandma touched her head lovingly, letting The Child know it was safe to take off running the distance to the cottage:

around the rocky bend, to the footbridge over the creek, past the split where one path led to the road to town, past mother's grave, then through the thorny gate to the path in the sheep fields to the little yard gate of the cottage. She knew the way by heart; she could never forget.

Grandma always knew her favorite dinner, mashed potatoes with anything, and she made them for her every time she came. They felt so good in her never full tummy. And there were always pastries in the big jar. And milk and butter from Little Cow and Other Cow. They often went to the garden together to dig the new potatoes right out of the ground, and there were so many other wonderful fresh things to eat from there and from the orchard, too.

"Wait for me while I do the chores, and then we'll go to the garden to look for dinner."

The Child smiled big and nodded, giving Grandma a tight hug. She went to look through her fancy trunk while she waited. In it were all the special things Grandma had made for her. She loved hearing her tell the story of when she was born, how she went home and started sewing them all, and she never tired of looking at them. Grandma said she was big enough to start wearing the beautiful dusty-pink cloak with the silk ribbon ties. She was going to let her have it on her fifth birthday in just a few days.

She finished looking through the trunk, at the beautiful cloak, the matching bag with the strap, the dresses, shoes and stockings. She sighed contentedly and put it all carefully back like she always did. Grandma usually came back in by now. The chores must be a little more difficult tonight.

Grandma had told her to wait. But it was taking even longer, and she was hungry again after the bread. She got a crisp, sweet pastry from the brimfull jar, taking small bites while going from window to window, pausing, looking for a glimpse of Grandma or Rowdy. Then she found her way up the steep stairs which also served as the pantry, tip-toeing between the glass jars which glowed in shades of yellows, pinks, reds, and purples, to the tiny attic windows for a better view, putting the last bite of pastry into her mouth. No Rowdy, no Grandma.

She decided she might just go over to the little barn to check. Grandma wouldn't get angry at her. She clapped her hands for Rowdy while she was on her way, and he didn't come. She looked all around outside and didn't see Grandma, but since the barn door was open, she peeked inside. Her eyes had to adjust to the change in the light. She could see Little Cow eating her hay in her stall next to Other Cow.

"Little One," she heard weakly. She saw Grandma lying down by Little Cow and Rowdy lying on top of her chest with his head on her cheek. She rushed to her side.

"Little One," she said faintly, her voice breathless. "I'm so sorry, I'm dying. See how Rowdy is resting on my chest with his head on my cheek? This is how he whispers that it's my time. And Rowdy is my Guardian so he's dying, too. I'm so, so sorry. I love you, honey. You can be my best helper now … and just sit with me …"

Grandma rested a moment.

The Child couldn't process what she was hearing. Inside her head, she felt like she was falling in a forever, dizzy spiral as she knelt down.

"I'm sorry I … could never take you to town … to Neesa … to the gates … for a Guardian …"

Grandma stopped speaking again to catch her breath, both arms around Rowdy, but now took one arm and with great effort, slid it over to her little granddaughter. "I hope you will still come visit my cottage. My beautiful pink roses always remind me … of you …" It was getting harder for Grandma to talk. "Don't forget …" her voice went to a whisper, "… the cloak for … your birthday …"

The Child's world was shattering like falling glass in front of her, like the day her mother's cut glass pitcher slipped out of her curious hands days before she had died, the shards spreading in countless pieces as they screamed out their destruction in a single roaring crash before her mother's anger rained down … She felt the same as she did back then, as if she couldn't breathe, that this is what it felt like to die because her heart hurt so badly; the pain was simply too much to endure. But she did as her grandma asked, not just sitting with her, but desperately laying right over the top of her, putting one of her arms around Rowdy so she could hug them both at the same time. Maybe if she held them both as hard as she could with enough of her body they wouldn't die; she could keep them here with her, stop the destruction of her world.

Yet only a moment later, her grandma lay very still. Rowdy also became still, and she couldn't hear him breathe anymore; he was always so noisy when he did. And Grandma should be talking to her. She listened. Horrid silence! She could only hear the sounds of Little Cow and Other Cow as they ate the hay Grandma had managed to put in their stall before she had sunk down onto the barn floor. She never noticed how loud the sound of cows could be as they ground the hay between their teeth. She grew more alarmed and tense as the chewing seemed to grow into a strange chaotic rhythm between the two cows, consuming the eerie silence that had overtaken the barn. She had always loved Grandma's cows, but now she needed them to stop chewing … *just stop* … *STOP* … *STOP!* …

The Child spread her little arms over her grandma and Rowdy a bit further, again holding them as tightly as she could, using her toes to push against them with a rocking motion to try to wake them, tears streaming down her face. She needed desperately to *hear* them, to have them stop the sound of grinding teeth. They still didn't move, so finally she sat back and looked at them, her hands tightly covering her ears, desperate to think of something, anything she could do. Things were so terribly wrong. There was too much to take in. The way they didn't respond to her touch at all. The pain in her chest was even worse now, pulsing with fire that ran up into her throat.

She needed help. There was only one place she could go, back into her original fear, the one that existed from birth. She retreated into herself, and pushing all her terror to one side of her mind, ran back to her house as fast as she could go, shutting off her tears as the afternoon sun was going lower in the sky. Crying made him angry. She burst straight in to her father, something she never dared to do.

He saw her dry, but tear-stained face. "What's wrong? Is it your grandma?" he asked, annoyed to have her back at the house.

She nodded urgently.

He set down a flask he had been holding and strode slowly for the door. "I hope you didn't do anything bad," he said gruffly. "I suppose you won't talk, even if it's to help your grandma, you're so good for nothin'."

She froze. What if her dad thought she did something bad to Grandma? She would talk if she could, but the words just wouldn't come out, they never did. She ran out to the woods to hide as soon as he left and silently cried until many hours later when she fell asleep alone in a grassy place in the moonlit night, exhausted, surrounded by the black silhouettes of the towering pines, and the noises of the night creatures, too frightened and broken to think of going home.

There were no words for such a child's despair.

7

Now that Grandma had died, The Child's father disappeared for days at a time, sometimes longer, leaving her to fend for herself. She often wandered down to stay at Grandma's cottage, passing by the graves of her mother and grandmother on the way, glancing at the stones which had been placed at their heads and feet.

She still was able to find a little something at the cottage to eat when there wasn't anything at home, but today, she hungrily ate the last dried out pastry from the big jar, as well as all the crumbs left in the bottom, and wondered what she should do. The man who had dug the grave had taken all the jars off the stairs and the baking goods from the cupboard, so even at the cottage, the only food left now was what was in the garden until the fruit came back in the orchards.

She sat down on the rug, alone with her new torment. Starting on the day Grandma and Rowdy had died, she was now cognizant of how their absence made normal, quiet sounds seem suddenly very loud. She never realized how many tiny creaks and pops the little cottage made all on its own. When she opened the windows, she was aware of the way the kitchen curtains sounded in the breeze as the fabric brushed against itself and the buzzing of bees and hummingbird wings when they were visiting the roses.

The trickle of the water from the spring through the kitchen board and down the side of the house seemed almost deafening to her as she decided to make her way to the chest of clothes. Her birthday had come and gone unnoticed by anyone, and she finally thought to open the trunk for the first time since that awful day when she had found her grandma dying in the barn. She felt a strange sense of foreboding she couldn't explain, as if something bad would happen if she opened it, but she made herself grasp the rim of the lid, close her eyes, and lift. The rich smell of the rare myrtle wood thickly greeted her, bringing back a brief flood of happy memories which caused her first to breathe deeply and relax, but then crumple to the floor in renewed shock that everything she loved was gone.

The percussive sounds of the water became more painful, and she clasped her hands to her ears as she stayed curled on the floor, but at last she pushed through the overwhelming sound, sat up, and looked through the contents of the beloved trunk once again. She knew she must go to the town of Neesa to find food because that's what the grownups always did, and that she should dress her best.

She took out a new pink silk dress, stockings, and shoes and put them on. Next, she took out the pink matching bag and strap, checking to see how it opened and shut. Then she carefully reached for the dusty-pink cloak with its hood and silk ties. Grandma had taught her how to tie the bow on one side of her face, and she did so now. The bright silk ties and lining made her deep blue eyes shine, her golden curls framing her face, and she held her little bag in her hands.

She knew that the grownups took money into town to trade for food. She didn't have any. The little coin jar on the kitchen board was the only thing her dad had taken from the cottage when Grandma died. She wondered what she could take in her bag instead to use for money.

She looked around aimlessly, finally going outside to look. She thought about rocks, but decided against them, choosing instead to fill her bag with beautiful pink rose buds. Since this was the best she could think of to do, she headed down the path away from the cottage, turning down the foot path she had overheard the grownups say led to Neesa.

Where the path met the main road, she left a rose to mark the place so she could find her way home, but then she had to decide. Left, or right? Did her right hand mean that right was the right way to go? She thought carefully. But if she came from a farm on the other side of the road, her right hand would mean to go left. So which was the way? Then she remembered her father saying she was too stupid to ever find her way to town if she was left on her own. But Grandma said she was smart, so she did go left on her own.

And at long last, Neesa came into view.

The busy market was full of people and The Child soon blended into the crowd. She had never seen so many people at once, and she felt very small and frightened, but her hunger forced her to keep moving forward with her plan, although she didn't really feel like she knew at all what to do.

A lady was taking some hot flat bread out of a domed oven, and fascinated, she stopped to watch her.

The oven was so hot it was glowing inside. The woman put the large, flat rounds of dough on a paddle and threw them one by one against the inside of the oven wall where they stuck, puffing up slightly as they baked. They began to free themselves from the hot surface as they finished cooking. Then she would take the paddle and catch the ones that were done, setting them out to cool on a table covered with canvas and dusted with flour. Her stall was covered in a shade, and the lady had a little red fox that slept peacefully under the table that was stacked full of the wonderful bread once it had cooled.

The bread smelled so good; it made her tummy growl and her mouth water.

When the woman turned, she spoke to her, looking down at her thoughtfully. "Look what a beautiful little lady you are! Shopping all by your-self, are you? Have you come to buy bread for your mother today?"

She suddenly didn't know what to do. Since she couldn't talk, she simply froze as she always did if anyone spoke to her. The baker kept working, turning away for a few minutes to keep the rhythm of the bread steady. The Child took a deep breath, again taking in the aroma of the fresh bread.

"I've never seen you before, what's your name?"

She was desperate for the bread, and she didn't know how to answer the question, and not just because she couldn't speak. And when she was afraid, it was hard to think. But she did think to quickly open her bag and hand the lady a rose instead of coins. She felt embarrassed, knowing it wasn't really money, but she didn't know what else to do but to pretend.

"Well, thank you for the flower, sweet pea! How would you like a sample of my bread?"

The Child quickly shook her head up and down; she never actually thought she could get something for a rose instead of money.

"Here you go! I can't sell this round, why don't you just take it since you gave me such a pretty flower."

The lady had a broken, misshapen flatbread and had given her the entire round. The Child was so excited she felt she could hardly breathe. She bowed her head in thanks, and not knowing what else to do, handed her another rose before turning to leave. The merchant was enchanted.

"By the way, I didn't get your name, honey. How about if I just call you *Rose* since you're all dressed up the same color as those pretty roses you're giving away?"

The Child smiled and nodded again. She liked how that sounded, and turned and bowed again, smiling.

The lady called out loudly, "Look everyone, the beautiful Lady Rose is visiting Neesa today! Give her a sample of your wares, and if she likes them, she just might give you a rose!"

The other merchants nearby laughed loudly, looking at the cute little girl in the pink cloak. The Child felt her cheeks grow hot at the laughter, but she now had food, so she did her best to ignore the uncomfortable feeling.

"Aww, Cleo, she's a cute one all right! Send her over here!" called Will, the fruit vendor. He gave her some bites of cut-up fruit from his stand on a little wooden stick. It was sweet and delicious. Will had a friendly shepherd dog named Timber that wagged and greeted her, and she patted him on the back before bowing her head and giving Will a rose bud.

Nearly all of the food merchants took turns calling her over. "Come here, little Lady Rose!"

One even gave her a sweet delight. She tucked the treasured candy that was wrapped in a little paper down in her bag to keep for later at home. She would save it for very last. Soon she had given away all but one of her roses. She had gone all the way to the far side of the Neesa marketplace and passed by the end of the crowds, pausing at a fenced-in place. Looking in her bag, she was giddy with excitement, her hunger relieved, and lots of bits of food left over. If she ate a few things from Grandma's garden, she could last a few days with only being a little bit hungry.

She also liked being called *Rose.* After all, Grandma said she reminded her of her beautiful roses. She got the idea that she would name herself Rose.

Rose began to look around at where she was standing. She felt happy inside, and she smiled as she looked through the pretty metal fence she was standing by and saw lots of bright green grass, carved stones, and beautiful flowers.

Looking further, she saw a group of somber people coming towards her, all dressed in black.

She chilled as she suddenly realized this looked like where her grandma and mother were buried, only much bigger. The procession stopped inside what she now understood was a cemetery, and Rose felt the familiar pain in her chest making it hard to breathe again. Her heart physically hurt as her own fresh memories painfully overwhelmed her.

Someone had died. She knew what that meant, and she knew how that felt. The horrible pain began to creep up her throat, yet she still felt drawn to slip inside the graveyard, noiselessly stepping towards the group of people who had now come to a stop surrounding a coffin. It sat inside of a freshly dug grave, waiting to be lowered into the ground. She listened carefully to what was happening as she crept closer.

She felt helpless and broken watching the people cry. With all the feeling in her small body, she wanted to make their hurt go away, to help them not feel like she did. But what could she do?

Everyone at the graveside now saw the little girl in pink silently and hesitantly finish making her way to the coffin, open her little bag, and gently cradle a single pink rose bud in the palm of her hand.

She kissed it, placed it on the coffin, and turned away, walking out of the graveyard, then down the road out of Neesa alone.

8

HIDDEN BETWEEN NEESA AND MATEO,

FAR BACK IN THE MOUNTAINS

SASCHA SENSED he was coming, though she didn't know exactly when. The Guardians always knew first. The little tan and white speckled chicken who cuddled by her while she slept was the first to awaken, popping her tiny head up and making soft clucking sounds to alert the others. Sascha's tabby cat, Ila Jane, jumped off the bed and stretched her back up in a high arch before rubbing around the blankets purring.

To get out of bed, Sascha very gently moved around Honey, a golden retriever who had recently begun resting quietly with her every night. She leaned over and whispered to her, stroking her fur gently. "Good girl, Honey, you're such a good girl. It's okay. It won't be long now. I'll hurry back, I promise."

Honey gave a small thump of her tail and feebly reached her paw out for more pets. Sascha gave in and stayed a little longer, stroking her silky fur and humming softly to her. The little chicken, Tildie, walked across the bed to Honey and settled lovingly on her, trying to mother her and keep her warm by fluffing and spreading her feathers over Honey's shoulder, lightly preening her fur. Honey again wagged her tail, this time to welcome Tildie, and seemed to relax.

"Sweet Tildie, thank you," Sascha said, stroking her feathers approvingly. "Ok, I'm coming!" she said cheerily to the many animals in her home as her bare feet touched the coolness of the smooth stone floor. "I guess today we'll start getting ready for our new guest."

Sascha was young and pretty, and she enjoyed her life with the Guardians. She marveled at how much each day was the same, yet also very different because that's the way life with animals is. Her routine had become busier lately; there had been more Guardians coming in recent years.

She washed and dressed herself, brushed and redid the plaits in her long, auburn hair, all the while petting and talking to the various Guardians who were her acquired companions. Then she checked over each one for ailments, getting them the individual breakfasts they needed, and giving them all some encouraging words. Next, she cleaned her little home that seemed to blend seamlessly into the forest. Just like the small matching barn, it was made of stone and logs, drenched with ivy on the corners, with a sod roof overhanging the doorway. Both were built into the side of a mountain at its base, safely hidden from the eyes of prying outsiders.

Next, she went outside to care for the larger animals with Ila Jane prancing at her side. There was the pony named Sam, the goat named Gustav, and the tiny donkey named Lily. She talked to them, brushed them, and gave them each a treat along with their feed and fresh water before going back in to check on Honey.

She paused, glancing down the mossy forest footpath, then shielded her eyes from the early sun with her hand as she looked up into the trees and sky wondering when he would come.

The forest animals all knew where the Sanctuaries were and assisted the Guardians in finding their way. But Sascha knew the importance of being there to immediately greet them whenever she could. Theirs was always a sad story, even in the best of circumstances. Guardians were devoted, and separation was devastating. They would remain at the Sanctuary until their previous owner passed, at which time, the Guardian also passed. Honey's time was close. She was in mourning to be with her former owner. From time to time, Sascha discerned some of the conversations between the Guardians about their former owners, what had happened to them, their deepest sorrows. The other Guardians would help Honey as best they could, and so would Sascha.

Ila Jane normally accompanied her during all her chores, but she had left to go inside the house. Sascha, noticing her absence, was concerned and went inside quickly, finding the house very still, and Ila Jane and two other cats along with Tildie snuggled on top of Honey now. Two of the other dogs lay on either side of her. Tildie laid her head on Honey's cheek.

It was time.

Sascha softly went to the foot of her bed and moved an everyday-looking blanket revealing a beautifully carved Realm's chest. She picked up a loose stone in the floor to retrieve a key and opened it. From inside, she first took out a small pouch she placed in her pocket. Then she took out a soft, white embroidered blanket, and a beautiful white pillow, filled with dried grass and flowers and endless scents from the Realm. The embroidery was of images of that beloved place all Guardians remembered, including the animals running free by the lake, and grazing in the large meadows.

She removed her shoes, because this was a sacred time. Carefully, she climbed onto the bed and approached Honey, reverently tucking the pure whiteness of the blanket all around her, gently in between and around her Guardian friends without disturbing anyone, so they could stay with her. Then she lay down in front of her, gently lifted her head and placed the treasured pillow underneath her.

Honey's eyes widened hopefully through her pain as she smelled the long ago but never forgotten scents of the Realm, joy now flooding her tired body.

Sascha stroked her head and spoke quietly with her head snuggled up next to Honey's, "Good girl, Honey, you're the best girl, do you remember home? Do you want to go back now? You can go back anytime you're ready."

Honey licked Sascha's face joyfully, thumped her tail once, let out one last, deep breath, then was peacefully gone.

And Sascha cried.

A few of the Guardians moved from nearby Honey to comfort Sascha.

While she lay weeping next to Honey, she took the little bag from her pocket and opened it. From inside, she took out a round jade jar, removed the lid, and took a soft wax pawprint from Honey.

Sascha gently smoothed her fur back in place as she set her paw back down, crying the entire time she did it. She replaced the carved green stone top and tucked the jar close to her as she continued to lay by Honey and the other Guardians.

She would later rise from her mourning and put Honey's paw print back in the pouch, returning it to the trunk before closing it, locking it, and replacing the key in the stone floor. At sunset, she would wrap Honey in her Realm's blanket along with her pillow and place her in a simple stone box that was next to the spring. In the morning, Honey would have been lovingly taken, and a new blanket and pillow would be back inside the locked trunk, clean and folded, the pouch refilled. The wax paw-print would be taken as well.

Sascha simply followed the instructions she had been given so many centuries ago, and she found comfort that everything was always in order.

And the Order gave her the strength to go on.

RROM THE GUARDIANS, Sascha now knew that
his name was Pippin. After sadly placing
Honey in the stone box and saying goodbye, she
once again looked to the skies and scanned the
treetops as well as the path. The sun was setting,
and though she knew that sometimes the journey
was long, she sensed that something was off, and
she wasn't sure why. Sharp breezes began to blow,
unusual, even for living in the mountains as she
did. She felt to make sure that Sam, Gustav, and
Lily were well secured in the barn for the night
after evening chores.

Ila Jane followed her back into the house, and
Sascha did her usual evening routine for all her
indoor Guardian friends, lighting her lamps so she

could finish, as it seemed to be getting unusually dark. She hung one in the window in case Pippin came in the night, and made sure the little outside welcome house was ready as well. There was a chance she wouldn't hear him right away because of sleep. It contained a warm bed, along with food and water, and a Realm's scented candle in a lantern in the eaves to comfort him. There was a Guardian's door into the house, but not all felt comfortable using it right away, so the welcome house was always prepared for new guests.

She looked outside one more time before retiring to sleep, still feeling uneasy. But seeing nothing amiss, and with Pippin still not in sight, she climbed into bed for the night after blowing out all but the window lantern. Tildie was there in her usual place, along with Ila Jane, and the fluffy black kitty named Minerva who sensed that Sascha was missing Honey.

The next thing she remembered was waking in the night to a storm ... not the usual rainstorm common on Placidéo, but something she had never seen before in all her centuries as a Sanctuary

Keeper. There were violent gusts of wind that blew the rain sideways in sheets, slapping the water against the windows and pounding all the water that was draining off the roof against the side of the house and against the door. Far up in the mountains there were flashes of light followed by long, low, distant rumbles which were occasionally loud enough to rattle the cupboards.

She got out of bed and lit her lanterns again, longing for light, grateful for the presence of her animal friends, though they, too, seemed uneasy, especially the dogs. They occasionally rose from their beds and went to the door, then turned to lie back down again, conversing with each other anxiously, and never quite returning to any sort of meaningful rest. The other animals behaved similarly, so sleep eluded everyone, including Sascha.

At last, the light of one of the moons breaking through the clouds seemed to chase away the storm, and Sascha had already dressed and done all the morning chores well before dawn. Pippin was not there, and by now, she knew he should have arrived. This was rare for a Guardian who was destined for the Sanctuary. She had put on her deep blue traveling dress, with its long, ruffled skirt, full draping sleeves, and red sash. She had also put on a deep purple fringed and beaded scarf she could use to veil her face from any curious onlookers. She gathered some needed supplies in her pack and called for Ila Jane. She blew out all the lanterns in the house, and as she set off, she was careful to latch the door behind her.

Outside in the darkness, Sascha checked the barn door as well. She picked up Ila Jane and held her close. The little cat purred loudly while Sascha petted her around her ears. Then looking into her eyes, she said, "Let's find Pippin. Show me the way."

She set down the bright-eyed tabby, and she pranced ahead of Sascha down the dark woodsy footpath illuminated only by moonlight. Her Realm's collar had a small bell attached, and it rang merrily when she was on a task, allowing Sascha to keep watch all around herself without fear of losing track of the little cat. But besides that, Ila Jane always came when Sascha called and never wandered too far away.

Even though the storm had been harsh, Sascha was still surprised to see the size of the broken branches scattered on the wet path, their large black shapes silhouetted in the early darkness. The wind had done great damage up close to the mountains. And though the storm was passed, she still sensed something uncomfortable. She had never seen flashes of light from the clouds before or heard such rumbles from high in the peaks, but this was not what she sensed ... there was still something more. She couldn't place what it was, but she knew she must stay focused on her assigned duties and not be distracted by fear.

Through the trees, Sascha caught a glimpse of a solitary eagle soaring towards the highest precipice, seeming to survey the mountains after the storm, as ever so slowly, the first colors of light appeared in the sky. She continued to make her way down the mountain, following Ila Jane's lead. Water leftover from the storm dripped *splat splat* from branch to branch, then to the forest floor, echoing ever so slightly under the tree canopy, and the cool air smelled fresh and damp as they walked. The birds began to sing cheerily as the sky lightened, shaking the water from their feathers as they hopped out of their damp, leafy shelters.

Coming off the mountain was rare for Sascha. Her Realm's cupboards were always full of exactly what she needed. The Order provided everything she and the Guardians required to live, and every morning it was simply there, appearing in the night. Occasionally, another Keeper stopped by, and these visits were always enjoyable, but all she really needed were her Guardian friends. Today she hoped she would find Pippin before anyone else saw her with Ila Jane, and that there would be no complications. Ila Jane didn't seem distressed at all, which was a good sign.

They were reaching the end of the footpath coming off the mountain. Ila Jane paused.

"What is it, sweet girl, show me?"

A flock of sparrows came and circled around Ila Jane's head playfully, and they told the tabby what she needed to know. Ila Jane turned left, the bell still ringing cheerfully in the damp morning, and Sascha followed. The woods were thinning a little, and they were coming to some meadows. Some sheep and two cows grazed peacefully, wandering out from under the trees to dry off as the morning sun promised to fully come out. Everything was looking familiar to her.

Then she saw graves and felt a wave of sadness. She now remembered precisely where she was. Time had indeed passed since she had been here the last time. She had an idea of exactly where Ila Jane might be going.

10

SAFEERAH FELT THE HAUNTING, distinctive vibrations and rumbles running deeply within Placidéo. Though countless millennia had passed, echoes of the memories she sought for now returned, memories of the days when there were great storms such as these, Placidéo herself mourning for peace, weeping for her little ones, the children, the animals, and the innocent who were in constant danger from the dark evils that existed on her surface. Great battles were fought to try to stop it, the wars no one remembered that only made evil stronger, before the people figured out the simpleness of the way.

But it had been so long since the Order had been established … since the words had been given that had dispelled the evil, taken away its power, and kept the peace for countless generations, that at last had protected the children and the animals …

Did the people not remember the ancient writings on the gates to the Realm?

11

Ｒose often went to Neesa for whatever scraps of food she could get now, taking her pink roses for trade. She always seemed to be able to get just enough to keep going, even though she was constantly hungry and getting gradually thinner. Most people thought she was the daughter of a wealthy local merchant or traveling trader because of her expensive looking clothing. Others didn't think at all, except perhaps to note that she was a cute little girl. They enjoyed getting an occasional rose from her and sometimes giving her a taste to try since she must be the daughter of someone they knew.

And besides that, getting a rose was a mock status symbol on many a slow market day. People liked to wear their rose buds and show them off, the men putting them in their jacket lapels, and the ladies putting them in their hats or in their scarves … such a fun conversation piece in a small village, with people cheerfully showing off whether or not they had gotten "a rose from the little Lady Rose." She never wanted to hurt anyone's feelings, so she tried to bring enough for everyone she liked, whether or not they gave her anything to eat.

With her Dad gone yet again, and her latest little cache of food nearly spent, Rose decided to gather more rose buds and go to Neesa for her usual attempt to stay fed. At dawn, she headed to the little cottage for her fancy pink clothing and her rose buds. It had stormed in the night, louder than she had ever remembered, with such a howling wind making things clatter around outside her house. The strange noises had frightened her enough to keep her from sleeping much, so she was up early. The violent weather had brought a torrent of rain as well. Water was still rushing under the little foot bridge as she crossed over it, and the path to the cottage was wet with puddles.

She changed into her pink clothes and sat back down by the trunk to close it. She paused. In a corner of the trunk in some lovely paper wrappings were the tiny handmade animals Grandma had sewn for her to play with. They were made to be just the right size so she could choose one to carry in her pocket whenever she liked, but she never did. She unwrapped each one, staring longingly at them for the first time since long before her grandma had died. There was a little tan rat with a crocheted tail and ruby button eyes. He was made with wool from Grandma's sheep. There was a grey cat, and a brown dog, and she had made a sheep out of the wool as well. There was a white bear made of fluffy fabric. He was made so his head, arms, and legs could turn using buttons sewn inside out. There was a brown cow just like Little Cow. And there was a bright red bird she especially loved.

But Rose never took one with her because if she chose one, she would have to leave the others behind. It gave her a lonely feeling to think of separating them from each other. To pick just one might hurt their feelings. So she always left them in the trunk together. Now she worried about them feeling alone in the dark trunk, but at least they were safe and all together.

Having no new answers, she shut the lid, leaving them all in the trunk again. This was a dilemma always heavy on her mind that she could never solve.

She picked up her bag and went outside. The storm had damaged many of the roses that climbed the side of the cottage, but after diligent searching through the thorny vines, she still managed to fill her bag.

Then she saw it. A beautiful bird lying still on the ground. Maybe the storm had blown him here. He had managed to work his way to where the spring water ran down the wall of the cottage where maybe he could at least have gotten some water, but then the rains had come, and he was soaking wet.

Rose was alarmed, wondering if he had died, and set down her bag, dropping to his side to look. He had deep blue and black feathers with a touch of purple, and a bright white chest. He looked up at her, trying to get to his feet. He was tired and wet, and one wing didn't look quite right, but now she knew he was alive.

Rose gently took her fingers and ran them over his damp feathers, wondering what she should do to help.

She thought quickly, then ran back into the house as fast as she could and found a piece of linen and a small towel, as well as her last bites of bread she had been saving for herself. She was afraid something might happen to the bird while she was inside, so she ran back out as fast as she went in. But he was still there, too exhausted to go any further, likely because of the injured wing.

Carefully, Rose sat on the ground and smoothed the linen onto her lap, then gently placed the bird onto it, wrapping him just enough she could hold him without hurting him. She offered him a bite of the bread, which he eagerly took. He ate several more bites before settling down into her arms as she gently and patiently petted and smoothed his feathers with the edge of the towel.

Slowly, he began to dry, his feathers beginning to fluff, and he let out a grateful little chirp. Rose was delighted.

Still trying to decide what to do about his injured

wing, some movement in the distance caught her attention. Looking up from the bird towards the path away from the cottage, she was instantly overcome with pure terror. A stranger had appeared on the path and was coming towards her. It was too late to hide. The stranger had already seen her.

She froze from fear as was her way, sitting on the ground in her pink cloak, her bag next to her, and the bird now cuddled against one arm on her lap. As the stranger approached, Rose covered as much of her face as she could with her one free hand, bowing her head towards the ground, but still trying to peek through her fingers, her heart pounding painfully.

"Hello there, little one!" a young woman's voice called.

Little One, she wondered inside. The term caught her attention just enough to distract her from her fear, and long enough to get her to look more closely at the face belonging to the voice, but it was veiled in a purple scarf.

Rose now could see the woman's eyes peeking over her veiled face. Her eyes looked kind, and she didn't look so scary now. She also noticed the woman had a tabby cat walking with her which she couldn't help but be curious about. Rose liked cats. She began to feel calm inside, now believing this woman would not hurt her.

"My name is Sascha, and this is my kitty friend, Ila Jane. I see you've been helping another little friend of mine. I'm so glad. He's been lost."

Rose sadly looked down at the bird, continuing to gently stroke his feathers. She had already grown fond of him. But then realizing that perhaps the woman would help him, she pointed at the wing.

"Don't worry, he'll be okay. His name is Pippin. I can see that you took really good care of him. May I hold him?"

Rose carefully folded the linen wrappings around the bird. Then she partially lifted the precious bundle up to Sascha who leaned over to take him, standing back up tall to hold him close to her face, gazing into the one dark eye that was facing her.

"Is it okay if I sit by you for a minute? We can help him together. Would you like that?"

Rose nodded, eager to continue to help the bird.

Sascha sat down on the ground and set the bird on her lap just like Rose had done. Then she took her pack from off her shoulder while the tabby cat rubbed around Rose. Rose held out her hand to pet along the back of the cat who started to purr, bumping her nose into Rose's hand to ask for more.

Sascha took out a soft, thick cloth for Pippin to rest in along with the linen from Rose, and they wrapped him up together, keeping him from flapping the injured wing and hurting himself more. The tabby came over and sniffed at Pippin, Sascha paying close attention to them. Then she looked back at Rose.

"Pippin says you shared your very last breakfast with him and helped to save his life. He is a Guardian. He has said so many good things about you. I wonder if I could share some of my breakfast with you?"

Rose nodded shyly.

Sascha reached further into her pack and pulled out several pastries just like her grandma used to make, as well as a perfect, whole apple, and she spread them out on a pretty pink linen. Rose was so excited to think Sascha might share these with her, but then Sascha slid the entire linen full of good food towards her. Rose felt her eyes widen with excitement.

"It's okay. I have more for me. These are all for you."

All for her!

"I was led here to rescue Pippin, and I need to pack him up and go in just a little bit so I can take proper care of him and get his wing feeling better. How I do that and where I live is a secret, but since you helped me and helped Pippin, I want to give you something very precious almost no one on Placidéo ever receives. It's very special. It's called a Guardian Stone. Remember to keep it always."

She reached into a small pocket sewn into her purple veil and pulled out a polished green tumbled stone that hung from a black woven pouch on a black cord. On it was painted a feather. She hung it around Rose's neck.

"I wish I could stay longer, but even though I have to go, I want you to know one more special secret to make you smile. I knew your grandmother.

I knew her as Savta. When I leave, go into her cottage and look at her kitchen board. On the wall where the water comes in, you'll find that one of the rocks is loose. Pull it out and see what you find. Goodbye Little One. Your Grandmother loves you very much, and I'm happy to say that you're just like her."

Sascha gathered her things, and she carefully nested Pippin in the top of her open pack, gently placing it over her shoulder as she turned to leave.

"Thank you again for helping Pippin," she called back to Rose. "Come, Ila Jane," she said to her cat, and the tabby trotted ahead of her down the path.

Rose waved. She gathered up the pastry and the apple into the pink linen by folding up the corners together and reached for her bag, getting ready to start back into the cottage, her curiosity about her grandma and her hunger for the pastry momentarily overcoming her desire to know anything more about the stranger. When she glanced up to look at them one last time, Sascha, the cat, and Pippin had vanished.

12

THE NEXT THING Rose remembered was awakening on the braided rug in the cottage feeling content and rested. The late morning sun was shining through the windows, and she had been sound asleep, so much so it took her a minute to remember what had happened. Or did she only dream it? Finding the bird early that morning, sitting on the rug eating pastry like Grandma made, and the shiny apple that had ended up tasting so sweet, feeling so wonderfully full.

Wait … she felt around her neck. There was the smooth green stone in its little woven pouch. What did the woman named Sascha say? Go look by the kitchen board. But Rose had fallen asleep. The storm the night before had been noisy and frightening, and she had been so tired and hungry.

She ran to the kitchen and began to feel the rocks in the wall. One was loose just as Sascha had said. With just a little effort, she pulled it out, and there was another black cord like hers with a pink tumbled stone in its own woven pouch. On it was painted a tiny black bunny shape. She knew that Grandma loved animals, too. And she had a Guardian Stone. She must have rescued a Guardian long ago as well. Rose took it from its hiding place and replaced the rock in the wall, and then put the Guardian Stone in her trunk among the little animals her grandma had made for her; maybe it could take care of them now.

Rose felt proud she was like her Grandma Savta. She liked the sound of her grandmother's name, and in her mind, she sang the name proudly to herself over and over instead of letting the loud sounds in the silence take over her thoughts. Now, when she felt her Guardian Stone around her neck, she felt that she would like to grow up to be just like her.

With her bag still full of rose buds, she decided to continue with her plans to go to Neesa. In her excitement, she had eaten all of the pastry and the entire apple. She felt so content to be full inside, for the first time, really, since before her Grandma Savta had died, but she still faced the reality that there would be nothing to eat later that day or the next.

Arriving in Neesa, she began her usual tour of the merchants, always starting with Cleo, the baker, Rose's favorite merchant. Cleo always told her she was the prettiest girl in Neesa, and Rose thought Cleo was beautiful as well. She had jet black hair plaited and pinned into a wreath on top of her head and always wore a white ruffled blouse with a dark skirt. She wore a fancy piece of jewelry pinned at her throat. Rose heard people say Cleo shouldn't dress so fancy to be a baker, but Rose loved how she looked. Cleo let Rose pet her little red fox named Skye, and Rose especially loved Skye's fluffy tail.

She also loved Will, the fruit vendor, and always went to him second. He made fruit pieces and would put some on a little stick for her to eat, just like on the first day she met him. She never saved the fruit for later. He said he didn't want her bag or her fingers to get messy, and that's what the stick was for, and Rose knew there was no way to get it home. He made sure to tell her that her rose buds were the happiest part of his day. Sometimes Will let her give Timber one of the dog biscuits that Cleo sometimes baked out of dough scraps, and she would reach up to pat the big dog on the head.

Rose's third friend was a tiny old lady named Marta who sat on the furthest edge of the market, so Rose didn't see her until she finished visiting all the vendors. Marta always held a cup out, and Rose noticed that people sometimes put a coin in her cup, so Rose always put a flower in it.

Some people weren't very nice to Marta, and Rose wondered if it was because her eyes looked funny, but Rose loved her anyways. Marta would always hold the flower up to her weathered face, taking in its fragrance, seeming to enjoy the smoothness of the petals as they caressed her wrinkled skin. Then she would feel for Rose's hand and tell her thank you. Sometimes Rose would share some of her food with Marta who would always say it was the best food she had ever eaten. Rose felt happy inside while she sat with her to rest before going home.

Sometimes Marta would talk to her when she wasn't trying to get people to put coins into her cup, just little things like the weather, or if people had been nice that day. Rose couldn't say anything back, but Marta always told her she was a sweet girl, and Rose always gave her a hug before she left.

Today had been a good day. The merchants were in a good mood for the most part. Everything had been washed clean from the storm. The colors looked bright, the air smelled fresh, and damage in the market had been minimal.

Rose had finished visiting all the food vendors and was sitting next to Marta after sharing some of the bread from Cleo with her, when she noticed another little girl who looked just a little bit older than herself. She was with two people who looked like maybe they were her mom and dad, and she was wearing a purple cloak that looked a lot like her own pink cloak. Two dogs were with them, and the little girl had a striped chipmunk she held in her hands.

Rose watched them, mesmerized, almost sleepy, sitting in the sun after her long day. The family went through the next row of vendors looking at their wares, the little chipmunk occasionally darting onto the girl's shoulders with quick, short movements, before again returning to her gentle hands.

Her parents smiled at her and spoke to her cheerfully, their interactions with her displaying obvious affection. They stopped in front of the silk vendor, and her mother held up different bolts of luxurious fabrics, holding each one next to her face, stepping back slightly to gaze at her. Apparently, this was to decide which ones would look best on her, and her mother caressed her cheek with adoration as colors were picked. Eventually, five different pieces were selected, her father smiling broadly as he opened his coin purse to pull out the gold pieces needed to buy the exquisite silks. Rose was fully alert now, watching the girl as her family left the shop with the expensive parcels.

They moved to the next vendor who sold laces, ribbons, and buttons, and mother and daughter took great delight in choosing matching trims for each piece of silk. Rose noticed how each parent occasionally kept one hand on the girl's shoulder, touching her lightly. Her father again pulled out the coin purse, attentively putting his hand on his daughter's head as he did so.

Rose had never more than glanced at these shops from a distance, because she came to the market solely hoping for food to survive. She watched in awe as the family all laughed together, speaking kindly to each other as they moved down the row. Now they went to the toy vendors and stopped at the doll-maker. The girl's father reached up and pointed at one of the most beautiful dolls in the shop, obviously so because it was kept in a cabinet behind glass. It was wearing a blue cloak with a matching silk and lace dress and shoes. The shopkeeper unlocked the cabinet with a key and removed the precious doll while once again, the father got out his pouch of gold to pay. Bending down, he placed it in her arms, kissing her on her forehead.

The little girl clutched the doll, closing her eyes for a moment in joy, then turned to leave the doll-maker's stall, noticing Rose for the first time. They fixed eyes on each other as the family moved slowly on down the row of crowded shops. The girl kept turning her head gradually further as she walked so she could stare at Rose until they disappeared out of sight in the throng of people.

There are ordinary experiences taken for granted in life that grab onto everything one thinks they know about the world and destroy it in an instant.

Rose was a survivor, and she was totally alone, but she didn't realize how alone she truly was until that moment when a little girl in a purple cloak locked eyes with her from across a market square.

The ache in her chest instantly intensified, seizing upon her. She picked up her bag without hugging Marta goodbye, running through the back parts of Neesa as fast as she could go. Her chest heaved in pain, and tears fell nonstop from her eyes. She didn't care if anyone saw her cry. Eventually, she found her way through the narrowest stone walkways between the smallest houses at the back end of town, then through the gardens and the edges of the fields, until she discovered the road that came back into the far side of Neesa. She didn't belong to anyone who cared about her or loved her. This was never going to change. She didn't want to live like this anymore, and there was nothing she could do about it.

Despite her grief and exhaustion, she was surprised to see that the road passed by a green meadow with a creek and trees next to Neesa she had never seen before. She had no time to notice any details about it as something else caught her attention … just past the meadow on the edge of the village … a set of massive gates. Could these be the gates her grandma told her about? … the place where she had wanted to take her to get her Guardian?

Overcome with yet another wave of loneliness and grief at the memory, she tiredly walked past the meadow, and having nowhere else to go, stopped in front of them, glancing briefly at the ornate work, then up at the bells so impossibly high. She could hardly breathe, her chest hurt so badly, and she started to break apart inside.

She clasped her little hands on the gates as if they were the bars of a prison cell, clenching them until her knuckles turned white as she slid to the ground, tears still squeezing from her eyes.

She didn't want to be forever alone. She now knew she would rather die. It would hurt less.

13

O N THE OTHER SIDE of the gates, Quill sensed the presence of a child who was all alone and in distress. He also recognized her as the witness the Emissary had spoken of. He quickly told Willow who began flapping her wings and honking furiously at the monks. Silas was close enough to Quill and Willow to know what they were saying, and he was already waving to some of the other monks to come join him at the gates.

Jarek arrived and was the first to reach for the rope attached to the heavy iron bar which locked the gates. He began to pull on it, lifting the bar to allow them to be opened, quickly doing as the Guardians insisted without ever having heard the ringing of the bell. Seeing the tiny fingers clasped tightly onto the upright bars of the ironwork, he tied off the rope and rushed to carefully open the opposing gate just enough to have a look.

Wags had now made it to the small opening and squeezed through, living up to his name by waggling his entire body, greeting Rose with as much enthusiasm as he could. To her, Wags looked so much like Rowdy, she allowed her hands to release from off the gates, reaching out for him in desperation. She silently cried over him as she held him close. Memories of her grandmother and her little dog at the cottage flooded her mind, bringing her torture, sadness, and a level of loneliness she could no longer bear. This was not simply a weeping child; this was a child who felt she was in too much agony to go on living.

Wags, always playful, sensed the condition of the little girl, and now held perfectly still on her lap, letting her hide her silent weeping face in his short, fawn-colored coat. She was in a little heap of paralyzed despair on the ground, covered by her pink cloak as she clenched the little pug with both her arms.

The monks could hear the animals saying she had come alone, that she had no Guardian, that many things in her life were horribly wrong. Her name was … Rose? And she needed to immediately be seen by the Guardians within the Realm.

Anyone over eight was forbidden under any circumstance. Fortunately, she looked to be about five years old, still unusually old to enter the Realm, but not unheard of. And of course, the monks never questioned the bidding of the Guardians, and they would do their very best for her.

"Come! Come little Rose! Welcome to the Realm! Come say hello to our friends!" they called ever so gently.

Then Silas tenderly knelt to be closer to her level, two of the other monks standing by his side. He carefully helped to ease her through the gates just enough they could be closed and softly said to her, "My name is Silas, and these are my friends, Jarek and Petra." He then patted the little pug. "Let me introduce you to Wags. He'll be your first friend." They ever so gently continued to coax her to her feet and ushered her a little further away from the gates and closer to the formal gardens.

The three monks looked at each other tearfully. They had never had a child come to them alone and in such a condition. Her despair was nearly overwhelming to their senses. They gave the Guardians a little time to begin their work.

Rose sat down again, weeping silently, and wouldn't let go of Wags, who continued to sit very still and let her hold him. Willow leaned against her protectively, softly draping her white feathered neck over her, and Quill came to sit down in front of her, watching over her carefully.

Saren and Gideon had now joined them, wondering what had happened. They could all sense Quill talking to Willow. Gideon voiced for him, "Quill is telling Willow she has come, that they must help her."

Petra softly chimed in. "It's all right, Rose, we're all your friends, and we're here to help you, just take a little time and rest with your new companions you've got with you there."

"She's mute," Gideon sensed, whispering it quietly to the others. "The Guardians sense she has a very pure heart, but she's all alone; there has been death, hunger, hurt, sorrow, and it's not going to get better."

Silas shook his head. "How can this exist on this world? Does no one know about her to help her?" he asked.

"We must wait to know what else the Guardians see in her. Perhaps we will learn more." Petra sighed deeply, her sorrow showing.

"She has a Guardian Stone," Jarek observed softly. They glanced at each other in mixed reactions of surprise and curiosity.

"So young," Silas whispered.

"It's okay if you can't talk to us, Rose," encouraged Petra. "Most of the children who come here can't talk except for a very few words, and it doesn't matter." She gave Rose a Realm's handkerchief with white floral lace and embroidered edges to wipe her eyes and nose, tucking it gently between Rose's little fingers and Wags so she wouldn't have to let go of him to accept the handkerchief.

Petra reminded Rose a little bit of her grandmother, and her tears began to slow a little as she still fervently held onto the patient little dog. She started to glance at the gardens; there were some roses and other flowers, and there were fountains that made the sound of splashing water. It all reminded her a little bit of the cottage. Her grandma would like it here. She began to think this really must be the place she said she wanted to take her but couldn't.

Petra interrupted her thoughts. "Would you like to take a little walk with me? You can bring Wags with you. He'll follow you wherever you go. I'd love to come with you." She reached a hand down to Rose.

Rose nodded and took the ancient hand that helped her patiently to her feet. Petra's hand felt cool and comforting; her skin was soft like her grandma's, and they began to walk down the gentle hill towards the lake, with Wags, Willow, and Quill walking contentedly by her side, the animals sensing they needed to be extra calm for this particular child.

When they arrived at the soft grass of the lakeshore, the beautiful Realm's blankets and pillows were immediately brought to her. A fresh set of soft clothes was also brought, and the precious things from her grandmother were taken to be carefully laundered and later returned.

Rose got to have a warm bubble bath, supervised by Willow and her duck friends in a massive tub behind a lovely white floral privacy screen, with white jasmine growing all over it. The jasmine gave off a sweet scent, and Rose liked the feeling of the warm water and the bubbles. She also liked the seclusion given by the white flowers; such a soothing change from what it was like having to clean herself in the cold creek near her house. Wags brought a little snack for her to eat, carried in little baskets on each side of his back, decorated with flowers all around.

Rose was granted the sacred gift of childhood play, and she had fun with the ducks who had their very own tub of plain water next to hers. She could throw a toy to them, and they would dive in their pool and drop it back into her tub. Then they would do it all over again. She was delighted.

As she played in the pure iridescent bubbles, the pain of her past felt soothed in the healing waters of the Realm. Her anxiety seemed to be carried away bit by bit with each of the bubbles that floated off into the sparkling sunshine, then vanished with a magical *pop*.

When she was finished, there were fluffy white Realm's towels to dry off with. There was everything she needed for after her bath before putting on the soft, flannel clothes which felt comforting against her clean skin, and Rose quickly fell fast asleep at the edge of the lake, with Wags and Willow cuddled close, Quill nearby, and Petra sitting by her, humming an ancient lullaby.

For the first time since Grandma had died, Rose felt truly safe, and slept deeply, perhaps more soundly than at any time in her life.

This was the Realm.

14

ROSE AWOKE as the sun was setting. The time between sunset and moonrise always sent a wave of fear and sadness through her body, though she couldn't remember why. Wags, sensing this, scooted over quickly to cuddle even closer to her. The Keeper friends she had made all came to be with her so she wouldn't be alone, and to gather as much information as possible from the conversations of the Guardians so they could assist Rose as best they could.

As the last of the sunlight faded and two moons began their rise, the monks told Rose to watch how the plants and flowers would begin to glow. Again, her fears eased as she became enchanted by their beauty. She then watched the spirits of Guardians appearing and pointed at them, smiling as they joyfully began to interact with the Guardians present. The monks rarely had a child old enough to explain such things to, but they felt it would be all right to tell her a little about what she was seeing and let her know that some of the animals were the spirits of the Guardians past and future.

At that very moment, Wags began to be very excited and greeted a spirit pug. They went running in circles of joy, round and round each other, stopping for a moment to sniff noses excitedly, then running in circles again.

Rose, after watching them for a while, breathed in sharply and held as still as she could. There was something about the second pug … Anxiously, hopefully, she strained to look more closely … Could it be? Wags and the spirit pug approached her excitedly, Wags, so full of his usual happy movement, but then the spirit pug paused, looking at Rose in what seemed to be his own amazement, before rushing to greet her just as brightly as Wags had done when he first saw her. It was Rowdy! Rose would know his little twisted nose and bottom snaggled tooth anywhere.

He came to a stop just in front of her, wagging his tail in a circle just like he did when he was with Grandma.

Rose became motionless as she could *feel* him send love to her. He was sending knowledge directly to her mind, and he could also tell what she was feeling and thinking. She could talk in her mind and he could hear her! *No one had ever heard her talk before.* She told him she loved him and Grandma and missed them. And he said to her mind that they loved her, too, and that they would all see each other again. She reached out to touch him, and she could *almost* feel him … she *could* feel him … it was just different … like he was only half there maybe. It was hard to think about it in words. He even licked her face just like he used to, but with this new kind of touch she couldn't really describe. Then he ran off to play again. And even though things didn't feel the same as before, she felt perfectly loved in a new way.

She now knew that Rowdy wasn't gone, Grandma either. She felt calm as she ate an evening meal. She felt safe, and her tummy was full, and after a while she drifted off to sleep again. As she did so, she wished to stay here *forever*.

At dawn, at the edge of the forest, a lone Emissary appeared, the majestic white horse who had paused to speak with Quill at the end of the last meeting of the Emissaries. Stopping further up the lake, she waited for Quill. Jarek, noticing her arrival, discreetly made his way to their meeting point to discern their conversation, reporting back to Petra after the horse and Quill had finished talking.

Quill returned to Rose, and the horse took her time, drinking from the fresh waters of the lake, resting in the meadow for a while before returning to the forest.

Jarek felt burdened by what he had heard, feeling yet more weight of the evil that had befallen their world. Taking Petra aside, he relayed the words the Emissary had given to Quill.

"The Emissary says that the evil has now come to Placidéo. There is still no more information as to what it is. It won't take Rose's life, but it will wound her deeply. We cannot interfere with the future and tell her about it. She must go back out of the Realm and fulfil her part. As for receiving a Guardian, it is obvious she doesn't have the means to care for one. Because she is pure and because she is destined to fulfil her part against this evil, she is to be granted The Realm's Gift, which means she will be given the deepest wishes of her heart. But sadly, it is because there will be a future time of great despair, when to survive this mission, she will need to remember she is to receive this compensatory gift, and to trust all that we tell her now.

Petra sighed deeply with the weight of this information. She and Jarek looked upon Rose sleeping peacefully by the lake. She looked so fragile and small. With what they knew about her from the Guardians, it was unbearable to think they would be sending her back out of the Realm to no one, back to a life of complete hardship and sorrow. Petra felt she wanted to wait a while before having to explain such news to her just yet. She knew this little girl would not want to leave the Realm, and how could they blame her, let alone explain it to her? She asked for a meeting of all Keepers before she acted on such a difficult assignment.

Meanwhile, Quill also quietly gathered a small, rather private meeting of some of his most trusted Guardian friends. It was decided that although Rose could not safely care for a Guardian, Twig would be sent. The little cardinal eagerly accepted his duty, hopping about on the ground in all his red feathered finery. He could fend for himself, and he would keep an eye on Rose from a distance, visiting her when it was safe to do so.

He now flew to Rose, and when she woke up, she loved him instantly, letting him perch on her finger and petting him gently on his fluffy capped head. He sang to her, and he reminded her of the little red bird her grandmother had made for her that was safely with the animals in her myrtle-wood trunk at the cottage.

The Keepers noticed that Twig was chosen, and their hearts took courage at the Guardians' wisdom.

They introduced her to Twig as her special Guard-ian friend, and they taught her how to whistle to get him to come to her.

Rose was delighted to learn that for the first time in her life, she could make a sound.

"Twig will be a cherished companion. You don't have to do anything to take care of him unless you want to. Just be kind to him, and he will always be close by you when you leave the Realm," Petra said.

… when you leave the Realm …

Petra saw the look of panic cross Rose's face. She realized she had broken this topic earlier than she had meant to. With her slip of the tongue, the meeting of the Keepers never took place. Sadly, it had just been Petra's way of trying to avoid the inevitable. Petra already knew what she had to do and simply needed to do it. She compassionately faced up to her duties.

"Come. Sit with me, Rose," she said, patting her hand on the soft pillows next to her. "It is the wish of many children to never leave the Realm, and I can imagine for you, that desire is more so than with most children. All children have a destiny to

fulfil, and you have a mission that is very important. I know you are strong enough to do it, just
like your Grandma Savta was strong, and in return,
you are being granted a very special gift called 'The
Realm's Gift.' Do you know what that is?"

Rose shook her head.

"It means you will be granted the very deepest
wishes of your heart. I promise. Those wishes may
not come as quickly as you hope, but I promise
you, they will come."

A mission? Rose could only desperately think
that the very deepest wish of her heart was to not
leave this place, so why did she have to go?

Petra sat with her for a long time by the lake,
holding her close and humming the ancient melodies like Rose's grandma used to do ever since she
was a baby. Willow took a brief swim and flapped
her wings, spreading droplets of water sparkling in
the sunshine before returning to rest by Rose. Wags
fell asleep on her lap listening to Petra, and Rose
absently petted his dark, velvet ears, remembering
Rowdy. Her mind gradually soothed, and somehow her spirit calmed inside of her.

The other Keepers had filled the rest of her little bag with as much food as they could. It was all they could do. They were saddened as they looked at the little food she had worked so hard to gather for herself. No wonder she was hungry. Her clothes had now been returned to her, and she was changed and ready to go. They were all feeling sad for her, but they had faith to do as the Guardians required.

"You must trust us, Rose," Silas began. "Even though you will still have hard things happen, everything will be different because you have been to the Realm. After you leave, it will all just feel like a dream, but remember what you have seen here, and it will all work out in the end. Whenever you see the gates, or think of the Realm, or your Guardian Stone, know that you're never truly alone."

Rose believed what she was told, but her spirit was weary. There was no way for her to ask if she could stay, and she was guessing there was no other way except for her to leave, anyways.

A new kind of sadness filled Rose as she walked towards the gates with everyone. The Realm felt like home. There was nothing for her outside those gates, but as they opened, each of the monks knelt beside her, quietly giving her words of encouragement and love, a few of them tucking little pink roses from the garden into the curls around her face. She remembered the little girl in the market and was sure this is what it felt like to be loved and cared for. Wags, Quill, and Willow were there as well, saying goodbye in their own way, staying as close to her as they could. Twig nested inside the hood of her little cloak next to her cheek, ready to go with her as she left.

As she stepped through the gates, Twig took flight, coaxing her little by little into Ermingild. Rose now remembered wondering about the garden and followed him with curiosity as the gates of the Realm ever so softly closed behind her.

15

BEING IN THE GARDEN reminded Rose just a little of being in the Realm, and she liked how the water in the creek came from under its wall, and how the birds flew back and forth over the wall. Even Twig occasionally went over the wall and back, making her feel like the Realm wasn't so far away. She sat on the grass and remembered Wags and Willow and seeing Rowdy, and she felt a tiny bit better being so close to it all. She remembered Silas saying to remember she wasn't truly alone when she thought of the Realm. She petted Twig as he rested with her in the grass by the creek while she gathered her courage to decide what to do next. Silas said everything would be different because she had been there. What did that mean?

Splash!

She heard what sounded like something big or heavy had landed in the creek. Startled, she jumped up and looked around. She was sure she had been alone, and she was nervous.

Kerplunk!

She thought she glimpsed someone behind the trees, but she was sure she hadn't been seen. She snuck closer and peeked. It was a boy, bigger than she was. He wore a cream colored woven tunic over his pants, and he had dark curls all over his head. His back was to her, and he was trying to loosen a big rock by digging around it in the moist clay soil with a stick.

He was putting a great effort into it, stopping occasionally to see if the rock was loose enough to pick up. At last, he gave up, turning his attention to a smaller rock, picking it up and throwing it into another deep place in the creek.

Sploosh!

"Hey!"

She froze. He had caught a glimpse of her. Realizing there was nothing she could do, she covered her face with her hands and plopped down on the grass.

"Who are you?" He had picked up his digging stick in one hand and was looking at her.

She uncovered one eye.

"What's your name?"

She uncovered the rest of her face and looked down at the grass where she had sat down, unwilling to look directly at his face.

Apparently oblivious to her fear, he continued, "I'm not from here. Are you?"

She brightened a little because she didn't live here either and shook her head.

"Me neither. Do you want to play? I like throwing rocks in the creek here."

She nodded, finally looking up at him, startled at his vivid blue eyes, much more blue than her own. She took off her newly cleaned pink cloak, setting it on a large rock, and they both began digging at the sought-after rock, eventually freeing it and hefting it into the water together. They stood for a moment just looking at each other quite satisfied and grinned.

"I live in Mateo. Where do you live?" he asked as he absently pulled a leaf off a tree.

She shrugged.

"Hey, can you talk, or do you just not want to talk?"

She suddenly panicked and looked frightened, shaking her head.

He saw her fear and quickly said, "It's okay if you can't; my mom can't either. She's really pretty, though. My name's Taavi. I still want to know what your name is."

She hesitated, then took one of the roses from her hair that the monks had given her and pointed at it.

He got a rather serious look on his face as he thought for a moment, then asked, "Is your name Rose?"

She nodded quickly.

He smiled excitedly and said, "My mom and I play games like that all the time!" Just then, a big white Great Pyrenees dog came walking up to greet them. Taavi patted him and said, "This is Zeke. You can pet him. He's my friend."

Zeke wagged slowly and Rose carefully reached out to the gigantic dog. He was surprisingly gentle, and Rose liked him very much. Zeke licked her hand before sitting down on the grass beside the two children.

Rose whistled and got Twig to land on her finger to show him to Taavi.

Taavi smiled even bigger, fascinated by the bright red bird. "Does he have a name?"

She nodded and pointed at a tree.

"Is it the name of a tree?"

She shook her head and grabbed a branch. Taavi seemed puzzled, so she pointed at a tiny portion of the branch.

Taavi furrowed his brows together, thinking. "Are you pointing at the leaves?"

She shook her head again.

"Branch, brown, wood, woody, bark, twig…"

Rose nodded big and grinned.

"Twig?"

She nodded again and Taavi laughed.

"I like that name! Hello, Twig!" And he gently petted the little cardinal with one finger. "He must be a really good friend like my Zeke."

Rose, Taavi, and Zeke spent a delightful afternoon together in the garden of Ermingild, with Twig flitting from branch to branch watching over them all.

Meanwhile, Taavi's parents, Léo and Tashi were managing their new outdoor shop in the Neesa market. Tashi had become one of the finest silk ribbon embroiderers in the region, and Léo was proud of her, working hard to make everything else in her life as easy as he could while she worked long hours at what she loved, and their shop was thriving. They now came to Neesa several times a week to sell at the market. Taavi knew to come back to them after mid-afternoon when they closed up their wares to get ready for their walk back to Mateo.

"I have to go back now," Taavi said. "Maybe we can play again. We come here a lot."

Rose smiled and nodded happily.

"Come on, Zeke!" He waved at her as he and Zeke began to turn to go.

Rose suddenly felt a wave of deep sadness, and Taavi caught the look on her face. He stopped and turned back to her. "Are you sad because I'm leaving?"

Rose nodded, surprised as the smallest tear escaped.

"My mom does something when she's sad about saying goodbye."

Taavi put his hands on her shoulders and positioned Rose so she was standing straight in front of him. He looked into her eyes, smiling, and put his hand on her forehead, then on his, then on her heart, then on his, and then he hugged himself.

"There," he said. "That means we'll always be thinking of each other until we see each other again, okay?"

She nodded and waved, and he waved back, as he and Zeke left Ermingild.

She had hope. Didn't Silas say her life would be different? She now had a Guardian, and she also had a friend. And she could whistle, which she did now, bringing Twig to perch inside her cloak as she left Neesa for the day with a full bag of food, and a mind full of things that had happened. She would think about her friend until she saw him again.

16

ROSE BROUGHT TWIG and came to Neesa several times that week, hoping to see Taavi, and happily, she did. She had never had a friend before, and she was relieved that he didn't seem to mind she couldn't talk.

Twig always stayed out of sight when Rose was around her merchant friends but was always quick to rejoin her afterwards in Ermingild. He and Zeke seemed to make friends as well, the tiny red speck of a bird hopping energetically around the giant white dog as he rested nearby the children playing, both of them ever watchful and faithful in their duties as Guardians.

Taavi knew how to make boats out of leaves and sticks, and taught Rose how to make them, too. They loved to run far up the creek to where it came tumbling from under the walls of the Realm, launching their fragile little creations, then following them together, running beside the rushing waters to see how far they would float before becoming stuck, or eventually meeting their demise.

Sometimes Rose would simply float flower petals and watch the waters take them as well. Staring as the bright bits of bloom would bob and float atop the sparkling water and glide smoothly over the shiny stones was soothing to her mind, allowing all her troubled thoughts to vanish into a peaceful place along with the flowing slips of color. The constant ache in her chest felt relieved here, and she could breathe more freely. She had never known this natural garden existed, and she loved to be here away from the burden of her memories and the daily stress of survival.

One day, as Rose and Taavi played in the garden, two travelers were coming into Neesa on the road that passed by Ermingild. The two men were rough looking and unshaven. They wore work clothes, deep colored pants with knee-high boots, and loose white woven shirts with full sleeves that were tight at the wrists. They each had a variety of tools hanging off their traveling packs and belts. Their heavy gear swung as they walked, making a rhythmic clanging as they kept up their steady cadence.

Zeke rose to his feet from where he had been sunning himself, eyes fixed on them steadily. Always panting from his thick white coat, he paused, closing his tongue up inside of his mouth, seeming to use the quiet to listen to them intently.

Taavi and Rose overheard bits of their conversation saying that the big storm that had hit a while back had made a rockslide partway up Neesa's nearest mountain. All the rain had caused it, so much so that a cave had opened up, and it really might be quite something to explore someday. They were wondering if there were valuable stones around there, maybe even gemstones, especially inside the cave.

Rose saw Taavi's face light up with curiosity.

He waited until the men had passed by. "Hey, Rose, you want to go try and find the cave?"

Rose felt an uncomfortable feeling. She liked the garden and felt she would rather stay. She simply looked down, playing with a tiny round rock with the toe of her pink shoe, then stooped to pick a little flower next to her other foot.

Zeke slowly walked toward the road, checking to see that the men had gone. He resumed his noisy panting.

Taavi pressed. "We have lots of time before I have to go back for the day, and I bet there could be lots of neat rocks. If we do find the cave, we can't go in very far anyways; we don't have lanterns."

Rose shook her head slightly, absently playing with the flower she had picked. She didn't want to go. She had never been to a cave, but she thought being inside one sounded scary.

Taavi paused, looking up the road for a moment before continuing, "Well, I really want to go. You can stay here if you want, but you really should come with me. I don't think it will be very far, and

I think it will be fun. Let's just try." He started towards the part of the road that turned away from Neesa. "Come on, Zeke!"

Zeke reluctantly started to follow. Rose decided she would go with them, but she felt more uncomfortable the more she thought about it. And besides, she was hungry all the time and didn't like thinking about using up all her food on a long walk. But she whistled for Twig who flew to her and climbed into her cloak for whatever this adventure would bring.

They had to walk quite a distance before finding a small trail that looked like it branched off the road towards the first big mountain.

As Taavi stepped off onto the path, Zeke whined and stopped abruptly.

"Come on, boy," he coaxed.

Zeke was a big dog and planted his feet firmly.

Taavi walked ahead a little, turning again to call his faithful friend. "Come on, Zeke!" he called, and patted his hands on his legs in encouragement.

Again, Zeke would not move, whining to show his disapproval. He tried putting his front paws down on the ground, back end in the air, wagging his tail slightly with a gentle growl before laying down the rest of his body. He was doing his best to encourage Taavi to come back to him.

But Taavi continued to coax, and Zeke obediently followed once again, not wanting Taavi to go alone, though he, Rose, and Twig began to gradually fall a little further behind him.

Taavi was eager to keep going on this new trail and see what was ahead. The storm had created interesting things to see such as large trees that had fallen over and gnarled exposed roots from the recent heavy rains. He was tempted to stop and explore such places, but the thought of the cave and the worry of running out of time kept him moving up the trail without stopping.

Nearly an hour had passed since they had left the road. Taavi was now even further ahead of his companions than he had been, and he came to a stop near the base of the closest mountain slope. A tiny brooklet was trickling down the hill, and he stopped to take a drink. None of them had brought any water, making it seem extra cold and inviting.

Though small, the flow of water had uncovered a variety of interesting rocks, and Taavi considered what the men had said. It didn't look exactly like a rockslide to him, but any doubts or questions suddenly lost their importance as something else caught his attention.

As he cast his eyes a little way up the hill, he saw a tiny sparkle of nearly blinding white shining in the sun coming from upstream in the brook. He was sure this was more than just the normal reflection of the water as it ran over the stones; it had to be something far more valuable. So he climbed, following where his eyes led him, up the slope to where it shone from under the water. Gazing down, he saw a gemstone, as clear as cut glass amongst the plain rocks in the brooklet. It reflected the sunlight directly towards him in the most brilliant way. He thought it must be a huge diamond. He couldn't believe his luck!

Bending over, he put his hand into the cold water to retrieve the stone, but just as his fingers made contact with its surface, it turned sparkling black. Startled, Taavi pulled his hand back to see if he was reaching for the wrong stone. It immediately turned clear again when Taavi let go.

Again, Taavi reached for the stone, this time pulling it all the way from the water and standing back up to inspect his find. As he did so, the stone turned to a dull, ashen, lifeless grey in his hands.

Disappointed, he dropped it back into the water in front of him, only to have it bounce upstream several times, skimming uphill across the surface of the falling water. Startled at its movement, he watched as it finally came to a stop under the water after the unnatural travel.

Taavi's thoughts on the matter were interrupted as he felt his attention drawn to a glimmer of color further uphill in the brooklet. A tiny bit of bright green caught his eye, even more impressive than the white gemstone he had just searched out. He quickly climbed higher, following the water's edge until he found it, unmistakably shining between two plain brown rocks.

Excitedly reaching into the cold flow of the water, he picked up the beautiful emerald colored stone and held it up to see it more closely. To his frustration, it again turned to the same ashen grey before his eyes. This time, he knelt back down so he could put the stone under the water to see if it would turn green again. It did not.

He stood up, holding the stone out of the water again, looking for any sign of the once brilliant green color, and seeing none, disappointedly dropped the stone in the water. It leaped from the water like a fish, skipping uphill many yards and landing upstream in the tiny creek just as the first stone had.

This time, Taavi felt an uncomfortable feeling in the pit of his stomach, watching as the stone had flown uphill in the running water, but again became distracted as he now saw a luxurious gleam of deep purple far up the hill. He felt drawn to go there, again remembering the alluring words of the men on the road. Had he found the way to the cave? Would he find gems there?

Up he climbed, sure that he would have a good outcome this time. He was high enough up the slope to now be surrounded by pine trees. Glancing down, he saw that Rose, Twig, and Zeke had arrived at the bottom of the hill and the three of them had stopped to gratefully drink the cool water. He waved, shouting excitedly as loudly as he could, "I'll wave again when I find the cave!"

But Zeke, seeing Taavi, was extremely anxious and not having it. He was whining and panting, barking frantically, now that he had closed some of the distance between himself and Taavi. He was doing his best to get his attention from the bottom of the hill with Rose and Twig at his side. Not feeling he was having any success, he soon left them behind, feeling an urgent need to catch up to Taavi, and despite his physical difficulties as an old dog, he began his climb up the steep slope.

For Taavi, the purple stone was also a disappointment as it turned into the same lifeless color as the others, and when he dropped it back into the creek, it, too, skipped like the others. It was as if it had a life force of its own, but even more powerful, this time leading Taavi's eyes to a huge, blood red, glittering stone where the small brook came out of the mouth of the sought-after cave, well hidden in the trees. Taavi was sure it must be a massive ruby and quickly took a step back to wave at his three friends before proceeding to the mouth of the cave to acquire the stone.

Rose had waited at the bottom of the hill with Twig, her small legs too tired to try the climb without rest, but now seeing Taavi disappear, presumably into the cave, followed soon after by Zeke disappearing as well, she began to get nervous about being left alone. Accompanied by Twig, she began to climb the hill after them. She had to take frequent small breaks, but she made slow, steady progress, following the little brook with its small splashing and gurgling sounds, up the steep hill. She tried to ignore her hunger, the midday heat, and the weak feeling she had from not having enough food for the exertion it took to make the climb.

She was so close to where she thought she saw Taavi and Zeke disappear, but she had begun to feel more lightheaded the higher she climbed. She couldn't see the cave. It should be here. She felt the need to sit for a longer break and found a grassy place to lay her head down for a moment.

The dizziness now began to overwhelm her … Something felt sickeningly wrong … Darkness … Her mind was spinning … Everything was in black and white, spiraling, even though her eyes were closed … Her stomach was sick … Fear … Total blackness … Where was the cave? …

17

THE NEXT THING Rose knew, she was waking up …

But she was not at the top of the hill by the brooklet.

She felt the coolness of morning air around her, the grass she lay on, damp with dew. Her body felt weak and sick. Twig was in his usual place, nested in her cloak by her face, gently stirring. Her pink bag that held her precious cache of food was still across her shoulder, and a small white puppy was curled up close beside her. Had she been here all night?

She heard a rustling sound. Lifting her head, she saw a great brown bear shuffling off through some nearby bushes. A tall elk, seeing her awake, pawed his front hoof, nodding his head along with his magnificent antlers before moving off into the pine forest.

She sat up slowly as she tried to figure out where she was. Nothing looked familiar.

She felt like something important had happened that she needed to remember … no … more than that … she had a feeling it was the most important thing that had ever happened in her entire small life … and she was *supposed* to remember it, but she could not recall what it was or anything about it.

She began to feel very strange and she sensed a great frustration building inside her mind. She needed to remember quickly. Whatever it was, she could feel it was so close, but she couldn't touch it, and the feeling began to torment her. Like something huge inside her mind was going to break open and flood everything in a massive wave of destruction, changing everything she knew, and she was supposed to open that door. But the door was lost. And the longer the door was gone, the larger the black torrents were that were forming behind it.

She lay back down on her tummy, hiding her eyes in her hands, trying to shut out the feeling.

Also, she hoped if she lay very still, the sick feeling she had in her stomach would subside. Exhausted, she fell asleep again, but only for a few minutes. As she awoke, she rolled onto her side, reached up close to her heart and felt her Guardian Stone.

The door in her mind appeared and opened all by itself … and pieces of the memory came pouring out.

She remembered being inside the cave, but she couldn't remember how she got there.

She was *terrified*, hiding behind a rock outcropping where she felt no one could see her, though she wasn't sure, and she could see Taavi, her friend. The cave was dimly lit, damp smelling, and he was sitting on something. He looked so frightened that his face was ghostly pale, but his blue eyes still pierced the grey chill. He was going to be punished for … taking a rock? *How did she know that?*

Rose didn't understand. There were rocks everywhere. She somehow knew the punishment was to be very bad. She had seen horrible things in her life, and she knew this was to be worse than anything she had ever known.

She remembered hearing a dog crying in pain. It had to be Zeke. She loved Zeke, and she felt broken hearing his cries, frozen in a desperate fear she had never felt before, sick from an unknown presence she couldn't describe. This was dark. This was wrong.

The crying stopped, replaced with whining from the pain, horrible pain, and the next thing she remembered was seeing Zeke dragging himself slowly, desperately across the cave floor, determined with every bit of his remaining strength to get to Taavi, crimson blood soaking through his white fur. He whimpered with every movement of his body, finally collapsing at Taavi's feet.

Taavi's fearful eyes filled with tears as he slowly, carefully reached one hand towards his beloved old dog, longing to touch him, to make one, brief, silent connection with his faithful Guardian who now lay wounded at his feet. He was terrified that even this slight movement would be seen by his captors, and he mourned that he had ignored Zeke's warnings. Taavi knew full well that something bad beyond his childlike understanding was about to happen to him, Zeke, or both.

Twig reached from where he was underneath Rose's cloak and picked at her Guardian Stone with his beak, and Rose remembered Sascha's words to always keep it with her. She remembered her friends in the Realm saying to think of them when she felt alone. Could any of it help? Also terrified to move in the slightest, she slowly reached with her hands hidden under her cloak for her Guardian Stone, held it to her cheek, and clutched it as tightly as she could, tears falling from her face, wishing for a miracle to save Taavi, her friend.

Just as one of her tears fell upon the stone, Taavi slightly leaned over Zeke, one of his tears falling on Zeke's head, and another onto his Realm's collar.

And then Rose saw and heard her miracle.

She could hear Zeke's voice in her mind tell Taavi, "I am your Guardian and I love you. I have found a way that you do not have to suffer this, but you must do exactly as I say this one last time. Be brave. Quickly stand up, walk to the light, and all will be well."

Right before Rose's eyes, Taavi stood up out of

his body; he was a grownup! He was shiny and beautiful. Rose watched in amazement as he stepped away from the little boy sitting on the ground, looking completely calm. After he took a few steps away from himself, he turned his head back to look briefly at the scene of himself sitting with Zeke lying bleeding on the dirt floor and then turned again and walked out of the cave alone.

Immediately, Rose was overcome with longing, even envy. She felt ashamed of her feelings, but she desperately wished to become a grownup, too, and walk out of that awful place. She wondered how he did that. She needed to know now.

This thought was quickly interrupted by a small, very frightened white puppy running for shelter between her legs. She slowly picked up the puppy to keep it safely hidden under her cloak, and her memories ended, waking up in this abandoned place in the forest, once again not having her latest wish granted for herself. Twig and the puppy were beside her, and she was still a little girl, alone.

The puppy seemed very sick, and she coaxed it

to eat a bite of food from her bag, then she gathered her things and headed down the mountain to find water. By afternoon, she had finally found what seemed to be the road back to Neesa.

While she walked, she worried about Zeke back in the cave, and she also wondered what had happened to Taavi after he had turned into a grownup, but most of all, she needed to find someone to help her make the puppy better. He was so soft, and he kept whimpering and crying as she carried him down the mountain, snuggling close to her face as she carried him as comfortably as she could in her small arms. He didn't look hurt, he just seemed very sad and in pain, and this made Rose stop often to pet him and kiss him, trying to love him enough to keep him alive.

After several hours, she hoped she was approaching Neesa. He had stopped crying and lay limp in her arms, although he was still looking up at her when she talked to him. Heartbroken, she hoped someone in the town would help her. She was completely exhausted and trying her best to get to the village in time to save him.

She was more certain than ever that the puppy would die if she didn't get help, and she was devastated at the possibility. Why did everyone and everything she care about have to disappear or die?

18

YESTERDAY

TASHI HAD BEEN tired today. Léo could sense it. He spoke to her softly, "You know, I'll be okay closing up shop by myself. Go ahead and go back home early if you want to. You can get a little bit of extra rest before tomorrow's market day." Holding her face tenderly in his hands, he kissed her on the forehead like he always did before cradling the side of her head affectionately against his chest. "Don't worry, Tash, I'll take care of everything and meet you at home tonight."

She kissed him back, touched her heart, then his, smiling as she turned to leave their market stall for the walk back to Mateo. Angel accompanied her on her walk home, spending part of the journey perched on her shoulder, other times darting off into the woods to explore, then reappearing on the road in front of her.

Though the walk was long, she enjoyed it when she could take her time. She always wore bright colored skirts gathered full around her tiny waist, light woven blouses with generously draped sleeves, and small embroidered slippers. She loved to be all alone and take off her scarf, letting her waist-length, thick black curls fly free. Sometimes, as she did today, she would hold her scarf over her head and dance a few steps in the middle of the road, turning, letting her skirt twirl like she was a little girl again. Tashi was delicately beautiful, and she remembered her many suitors, how their interest immediately waned when they learned she could not speak, but Léo had always loved her from the moment he saw her in second school. He sensed her intelligence, and he always seemed to know what she was thinking. She was so happy when her papa said yes to Léo's proposal for her hand.

Tashi continued walking as the road wound through shady woods of leafy trees and towering pines, past small farms with long rows of berries, vineyards, orchards, and small gardens. There were natural grasslands, as well as fenced-in pastures with peaceful farm animals grazing. A river ran along parts of the road, providing water and places to cool off on the long walk to and from Neesa. And halfway home, there was the Lovers' Tree.

Unknown generations ago, on the side of the road, two young lovers had braided three crimson maple saplings together as a symbol of their love. The trio had now grown into a massive, ancient tree. Tashi loved to walk beneath its vivid red canopy every time she passed by. She would think of the three saplings forever intertwined, and it reminded her of how much she loved her own little family which was now three. When she had time, she would sometimes stop and run her hands over its smooth bark, admiring how the three had woven into one so beautifully. She did so today, sighing in deep contentment before again continuing her walk home.

When she got there, she would rest as planned and then make sure Léo and Taavi had something good to eat when they arrived along with Zeke, Jett, and Angel.

Léo worried when it was time to close. Taavi and Zeke did not come back. Tashi always left them in Neesa when she went home early. On the rare occasions when she did take them with her, she made a point to tell him, but there was no way to know for sure without going all the way home. This obviously would take too much time. Tashi was extra tired. Could she have forgotten to tell him?

He felt genuinely conflicted as he tried to decide what he should do next. She would worry if he didn't come home, but he also felt he needed to be here in Neesa in case Taavi showed up late. He finally decided to ask the shopkeepers who sold linens next to his market stall to watch for them, as they were staying overnight in their store. They assured him they would watch for the boy and the dog, and Léo anxiously headed home to Mateo, gradually quickening his steps as he walked, starting to doubt his decision. Maybe he should have tried looking for them instead. His anxiety forced him into a run the rest of the way home.

Exhausted, Léo reached his house in Mateo, and fear seized his heart as he inquired of Tashi about Taavi's whereabouts. Tashi's face went pale as she shook her head, desperately reaching for her slate. *No, I would have told you.* Both their hearts broke as reality began to sink in as deeply and quickly as the last rays of the sun over the horizon. Tashi had already made dinner for them all. She pleaded, writing on her slate that she wanted to pack up their dinner and go back to Neesa with Léo, but he reminded her she should be home in case Taavi came there late. He would go back to Neesa immediately to see if Taavi had come to the market stall. Tashi felt frantic but knew in her heart this was the wisest choice.

Léo informed several neighbor friends of their situation as he got ready to leave, asking them to keep an eye out for Taavi, and to watch over Tashi. The men of Mateo reasoned with Léo, driving him further into his fear, convincing him they should not wait, that they should begin to search Mateo tonight. They said Taavi could have followed Tashi home, and they began getting ready. They did their best to prepare torches and lanterns, unusual for Placidéo, where it was customary to rely mostly on moonlight when outdoors at night, as they never had emergencies. Some of them chose to go back to Neesa with Léo to get the search going there if Taavi had not returned. A few of the women came to sit with Tashi, who was now beside herself with fear and also frustration, feeling she was doing nothing to help.

Most of all she wanted to be with Léo at a time like this, beside him, working to find Taavi. She needed to know that at her worst moments of discouragement, he would lean her head against his chest and hold her … like he always did, telling her everything would be okay. The image of the Lovers' Tree flashed through her mind … She and Léo so in love, and now their little Taavi that had made them three, her little family that had been all she had ever wanted. Getting them all back together was now her very life's breath.

As Léo stopped by their door one last time to say goodbye, Tashi went to her work basket and pulled out two bright blue ribbons, bright blue like Taavi's eyes, and gave one to him. Then urgently she wrote on her slate. *If he comes here first,* she erased, then continued, *I'll tie this on the door.* Again, she erased and wrote as quickly as she could, *and we'll meet you in Neesa.* Her tear-filled eyes pleaded with Léo to agree.

He grasped her by the shoulders, holding the other ribbon, and told her, "Yes, Tash, we won't be confused again. I promise we'll find him, and if I find him first, I'll tie this around the corner of the market stall and send someone for you. I'll wait for you in Neesa. I'm sure he's there already, and it's just a misunderstanding. People back at the market stall are watching for him now. We'll all get back together soon, I promise you."

He went to turn away from her to leave, and she reached for his face with both her hands, cradling his face, like he so often did to her, looking up into his eyes, searching, wanting to hear his voice say just once more what she wanted to hear.

Her tenderness, her vulnerability, her love and complete trust in him tore at his heart. He loved her more than his own life. He didn't have words for this love he had for her, had always had for her. She was the one who couldn't speak, yet she left him speechless. His voice was starting to choke. He wanted to be strong for her.

"I love you, Tash. I *will* find him."

And he tenderly slid her hands off his face, kissed them, and turned, leaving before she could see him weep.

Upon reaching Neesa late that night, Léo learned the nearby shopkeepers hadn't seen Taavi or Zeke. The last shreds of denial that gave him hope were now being mercilessly ripped away. His world was falling apart, and he had no control over it. He felt sick inside, and felt the wild, frantic urge to be everywhere at once in the growing search but could not.

The men from Mateo and the Neesa shopkeepers spread word, pounding on door after door through the entire town alerting everyone that Taavi was missing. Though already late at night, all the townsmen searched the village by moonlight, torches, lanterns, and even candles, desperately trying to find the missing little boy, the shouts of his name punctuating the night until morning, when plans changed.

At dawn, satisfied that Taavi was not in Neesa, organized searches began so they could spread out far beyond the town, scouring lakes, fields, up and down all the rows of crops, and everywhere they could as they thoroughly looked in farms, rivers, woods, anywhere a little boy might wander. More volunteers came from Mateo and joined as they finished their search, as well as men from several other villages. Everyone was questioned. All morning and into the first part of the afternoon everyone looked, and nothing had turned up even the slightest clue of where Taavi was. Exhausted, no one could think of anywhere else to try. It was as though he and Zeke had simply vanished. No one ever found the cave or the path to it to even consider searching them; both had vanished as well.

No one worked harder than Léo. He was the father. He was the provider. He would keep his promise to Tashi and bring Taavi home. It was his job to *fix this*. He didn't just pound a door, he slammed his fists into them, as though imprinting his soul into the wooden planks. He looked in places where Taavi could never fit. He wept, and he shouted Taavi's name. He used his entire body to *rip* and *shred* through fields and rivers with all his strength.

Finally, he saw a brush pile by a lake. Seeing a glimpse of white deep inside of it that he thought was Taavi's tunic, he *tore* into the thorny thicket with his bare hands like a ravenous animal, oblivious to the pain as its spikes deeply gouged into his hands, arms and legs, blood showing through his clothing. He was sure he had found his son. Suddenly, the white mama goose who had been hiding her nest in the bottom of the giant thicket came flying into his face, her feet tearing the flesh on his scalp and forehead in startled fear during her escape.

Léo flew backwards in pain and surprise, tripping on his heels and falling on his back, the attack finally bringing him back to himself as blood ran down into his eyes. He began screaming repeatedly in a rage that echoed off the mountains surrounding Neesa, his voice gradually giving out into rasping sobs before exhaustion softened it further into nothing more than the weeping of a father for his son.

By now, a large number of the men had gathered around him … waiting. They were strong, good men … and they knew … they were waiting for him to know, too. They waited compassionately, standing in a silent fortress around him, for as long as Léo needed to be able to finally say it, because that's what good men do … and when at last he said it, he did so in a quavering, wailing, childlike cry that rose to the heavens …

"Taavi is gone."

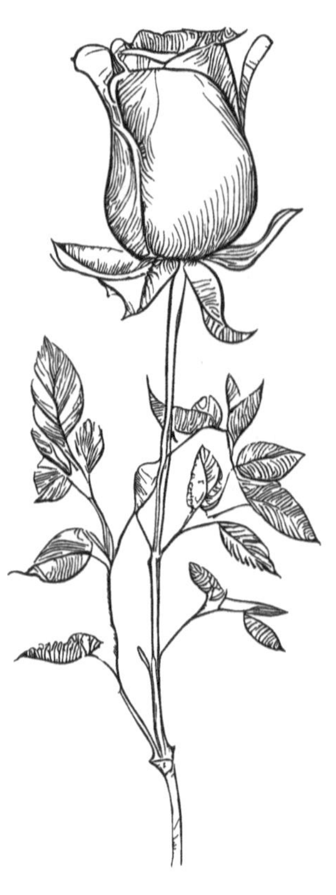

19

THE SAFEERAH LILIES felt a great sorrow outside of the Realm. She felt an overwhelming desire to reach her roots through the soil to find this weeping, so she began to stretch much further than she had in many millennia, perhaps ever, putting all her strength into a single root and extending it, all the way under the ancient Realm walls, searching.

20

Much later in the afternoon, with the help of Twig, Rose finally saw Neesa come into view. Her arms and chest ached, her feet were blistered and sore, and she was desperately thirsty and hungry. Her mouth and throat were dry, and she still felt sick from this morning, but she was determined to save the puppy.

Things didn't look the same as usual as she walked into the far end of the town, especially in the market. It looked mostly closed down, and Rose wondered where all the shopkeepers were. She quickly figured out that everyone was looking for Taavi.

She couldn't tell them. She had no reason to think they would believe her even if she could …

She didn't know where he went after he turned into a grown-up. She did hope he somehow got Zeke out of the cave later, but she couldn't remember anything else, and her mind was too weary and hurt to do anything except to try to find help for the puppy.

She looked down at him sadly. He was warm and still breathing, but he didn't open his eyes anymore. She was such a sad picture as she walked, trying to cuddle him up to her cheek, the bottom half of his body hanging limply down. Desperate for help, she walked up behind a familiar looking person in the street and ignoring her fear, timidly tugged on his jacket.

He turned around, looking down at her, and asked rather shortly, "What do you want? No one could find that little boy, and we've all headed home. You haven't seen him, have you?"

Her exhausted mind couldn't cope with two questions at once, so she simply pointed at the puppy, pleading with her eyes.

The man shook his head and resumed walking, hardly looking at the little creature next to her cheek.

Rose felt a severe pang in her chest. The rejection had stung deeply when she had to gather so much courage to ask for help. Images of her past flashed through her mind ... Grandma and Rowdy dying on the barn floor ... running to her dad for help ... staying in the woods alone all night ... terrified to go back home.

She held onto the puppy and pushed the images down. Her emotions were already shattered from everything she had experienced the day before, and she felt she was losing the strength to keep trying, like her mind was going numb.

But she resolved to keep going, feeling as though the puppy was the only friend she had left besides her beloved Twig. She had been carrying him for so many hours that her arms burned, and she now tried shifting how she held him, holding him like a sleeping doll in her arms. The movement helped to bring her mind solidly to the present. She checked him ... *still breathing* ...

She forced herself to walk further down the market street until she found another food vendor friend in a purple dress, and she tugged at her clothing more frantically, not waiting for questions, pointing at the puppy.

"Ah, look at that, Rose, you have a puppy. I'll have a look at him another time. We couldn't find Taavi, honey, it's been a hard day." The lady turned, walking away quickly.

Rose felt delirious watching the purple dress walking away. In her mind, the dress kept turning into a purple cloak, the lady turning into the little girl with the nice family that loved her, walking away in the market crowd, reminding Rose she was alone forever. She needed to run!

Twig rustled inside her hood, bringing her back again. She needed to check the puppy … *still breathing* …

The street was looking almost completely deserted … *look left … look right … look down the street* … There weren't many people left. The pain in her chest began to pulse with the beating of her heart. She was feeling so … alone … didn't the lady understand another time might be too late?

She was so exhausted she was becoming wooden. She must save him.

… check the puppy …

… still breathing … she felt tears down her face *… was she crying?* … the pain in her chest was starting to creep all the way up her neck … another person appeared further down the market square … she ran to them … *hurry …*

"Not now, Rose, it's been a hard day, another time."

Check the puppy … still breathing … more tears … the tiny pink slippers now panicked, running the length of the market street to its end … *I must find someone … anyone …*

One final person appeared … would he help?

"Later, Rose, we're all going home."

No one was left …

She was alone …

The sun was setting …

The street was now eerily silent and bathed in deep orange light, the time of day that depressed her for seemingly no reason. Everyone had gone home early. Even old Marta was gone. Rose sat on the street where Marta would normally sit next to her, too exhausted to go another step, the pain in her chest now screaming with every breath she took.

She felt the puppy still warm in her arms. She held him close, kissing him, cradling him with all the love she had, quietly pleading in her mind for him to live as tears dripped on his soft, white fur. Now that she was sitting, she took time to trace her finger along his velvet ears and tiny black nose. How she longed to be able to speak to him, to tell him she loved him, to hum the melodies she remembered from her grandmother, but of course, she couldn't. Twig now quietly settled in on the puppy's cheek, fluffing out his feathers and being very still.

... a breath ...

... pause ...

... pause ...

... a breath ...

21

ÉO WAS ILL.

Collapsed on their bed with unspeakable grief and exhausted from the futile search, and after finally falling asleep, he still cried out, because even the deepest slumber does not shelter one like this from such agony. Jett cried softly at the foot of the bed, unwilling to leave him.

Tashi was also sick with her own grief, as well as her helplessness to comfort Léo. Her loneliness for their son came in inconsolable waves, and as the sun began to lower, she inexplicably started toward Neesa without waking Léo. She remembered how she missed Taavi when he was a just a tiny boy visiting the Realm but also remembered the peaceful feeling she had in the nearby garden while she waited for him. She felt strangely and desperately drawn to go there tonight.

Night fell as she walked, and as she finally drew closer to Neesa, she remembered when Taavi came through the gates with the great white dog, how surprised everyone was to see such an old Guardian, but Zeke had been perfect for him, perfect for their entire family. Jett and Angel got on so well with him, and the little family loved watching them all play together. He couldn't have been a better match, really. She always felt she could completely trust Zeke to watch out for Taavi. And now Zeke was missing as well.

Where was Zeke? The thought unleashed a new torrent of tears. Her mind sunk once again into the same unending circular depths of desperate thoughts as she wept and walked.

Were they both dead? Or hurt? Was Taavi crying out for her? Did he wonder why she didn't come for him? How could she go on not knowing, but she must! He might come home someday. He would need her if he ever did. Or would she never know what happened? Was there somewhere else to search? Was there someone the searchers hadn't talked to yet? If he was dead there would be no grave … but he might be alive …

The embers of evil had scorched where they had landed, and Tashi's mind could not get past these hopeless, repetitive, maddening thoughts … the cruelest torture! Because she knew Taavi *existed* there … that's where she would finally find him! … just past these thoughts. She *knew* if she thought hard enough, he was just one thought away. Everyone knew it. Nature knew it. The Universe knew it.

But the very evil that had cast itself upon the innocent was the one that held captive that thought, throwing further embers of deceit that there would ever be resolution, justice, or victory. And just like the sun and the moons eternally pursued each other in the heavens and would never meet, it seemed she would be forever left searching for Taavi.

And then, in an occurrence that rarely happens on Placidéo, the third moon set, and the blackness fell as deeply as Tashi's despair as she softly tread near the gates of the Realm.

But her spirit pulled her even more strongly

towards the garden. Following the familiar sound of the water, she carefully made her way through the darkness past the gates towards the creek and into the edge of the garden. She knew it by the feel of the grass under her slippers, the sound of the wind in the leaves, the smell of the blossoms, the trees, and the water. She sat down, letting the night-time sounds begin to finally replace some of her futile thoughts. She began to be aware of the crickets, and the calls of a few night birds from a distance. Her body was tense and tired, and she pulled her knees up to her chest and rested her forehead for a while, just listening, remembering Taavi.

At last, the first moon began its rise, bringing welcome light to the darkness and revealing a misty, grey landscape. Thick layers of patchy fog were covering the creek and drifting down over large parts of the entire meadow. To her wonderment, she noticed a bright, white figure emerging from the mist who approached her from further down the garden.

Tashi arose and watched as the figure came closer, and she was able to see the features of a beautiful young woman … could she be an angel?

… She was light and shining in the moonlight. She was lovingly cradling a small, white animal in one arm, gently stroking its softness with the hand of the other … a lamb maybe? Or a rabbit, or a puppy? Tashi couldn't tell.

The angel paused, reaching up as if to gather the mist with her free arm, gracefully bringing it to the ground in a circular motion. Silver Safeerah lilies rose from the ground to meet the graceful movement. She did this several times until she had made a soft bed out of the wispy fog and gently laid the little animal down inside the moonlit layers she had created, smoothing its fur lovingly as she did so, and kissing it on top of its head. The silver lilies surrounded the beloved little creature. One of the lilies grew silver tendrils that reached up longingly for the angel's hand. She picked it gently, taking it to her heart before again rising to gracefully approach Tashi.

She stopped in front of her, looking at her with great tenderness, and as she did so, Tashi felt filled with a love she had never felt before. The angel handed Tashi the lily, and as its stem touched

Tashi's fingertips, the petals turned blood red, and the blossom began weeping from its center, feeling Tashi's grief.

The angel paused sadly, taking hold of Tashi's hands as she held the lily. Then thoughtfully, as she looked into her eyes, she touched Tashi's forehead, then her own. Then Tashi's heart, then her own. Then she put her arms around herself to show an embrace. Tashi felt warmth start both at her forehead and her heart where the angel had touched her. The warmth filled her whole body, and she took her first true breath since Taavi had disappeared.

Tashi's lily turned snow white as the angel smiled lovingly and turned back to pick up the little animal she had left behind. As she did so, the rest of the ring of silver lilies turned white and vanished under Ermingild's soil, and the angel disappeared into the mist of the creek where it ran under the wall of the Realm.

Tashi gently breathed in the cool air, staring for a little while at the mist near the wall, before turning to start her long walk home in the moonlight, holding the delicate frost-white lily.

When she was halfway home, Angel found her, scurrying up her shoulder to cuddle next to her heart, and Jett barked to alert Léo that he had found Tashi.

Tashi and Léo collapsed into each other's arms, falling down to weep together in the dark road to Mateo in the moonlit shadow of the Lovers' Tree.

22

But Safeerah waited in Ermingild. There were things not completed, things she needed to know, precious things she needed to watch over during the night.

23

ARLY IN THE MORNING, a passing traveler saw a peek of pink fabric through some trees just outside of Neesa. Curious, he left the road and soon could see what looked like a beautiful little girl in pink, fast asleep amongst some fragile pink wildflowers, all alone. She was curled up next to a rushing creek, a little ways down from where it flowed from underneath a great stone wall. She looked surreal, just like a doll, with golden curls peeking out of a dusty-pink cloak.

He felt mesmerized at the scene, and at the same time, somewhat ill at ease to see she was all alone, and he felt he should check to make sure she was all right. As he approached, he saw she was clutching a handful of deep pink roses near her face. Coming closer, he was overcome with horror and grief as he realized she had passed away, with a little red cardinal who had also passed, cuddled against her pale cheek.

The little bird was nested on top of a pink silk bow which tied the hood of her cloak on one side, framed by the roses in her hand. In her other arm was a small white puppy, a Great Pyrenees. It, too, was deceased, cuddled up inside the curve of her small body. The little girl looked so thin and tired, like she had just given up and laid down to sleep, never to awaken again. The man turned and ran into the town without daring to disturb her resting place, weeping in a state of shock, calling out to alert everyone of his sad findings.

The people of Neesa rushed to the creek, immediately recognizing the traveler's description as little Rose before ever arriving at her side. Questions erupted. Why was she so thin? Didn't anyone notice before? Where were her parents? Surely someone knew. Maybe she was from Mateo. But in the end, it seemed no one knew.

And no one came asking for her.

She was buried next to the creek before sunset in her little pink dress and shoes, and her matching pink bag, and her dusty-pink cloak and hood, with her roses in her hand surrounding the little red cardinal tucked by her cheek and the puppy tucked in her arm, just as they all had been found. A small, green tumbled stone with a painted-on feather was in a little woven pouch on a cord around her neck.

The people in the town all gathered and some brought small gifts to place with her before lowering her gently into the ground, remembering all the times the little girl had shared roses with them as gifts and how happy she looked when she gave them away.

Cleo brought her the brooch she always wore; she remembered how Rose especially liked it. She had been her friend.

Some people offered another kind of gift by offering to take care of people and animals they now knew Rose had loved.

Blind Marta came and cried about Rose, and the people hugged her. She told them that Rose had shared her food with her and the people now knew that Rose had been starving when she had done it. So Will and a group of people decided that they would take care of Marta to remember Rose.

Others remembered how much she loved animals and was kind to them, so many resolved to be more caring and kind to their animals.

… but some remembered with the deepest sorrow of them all, that she had been asking them for help for the puppy, and they had brushed her aside. They now knew that sometime just after that, she and the puppy, along with the little bird, had died alone … this was unspeakable sorrow … too much to bear.

… These were the broken ones … the ones that felt as if they no longer belonged in their village circle, too paralyzed by shame or pain to speak of what had happened, the ones who felt unworthy … the reasons didn't matter.

And the villagers searched them out and comforted them as well and brought them back into their circle. They said that Rose would have wanted it. And that they wanted it, too.

Let there be no more lost ones.

The townsmen then found two beautiful pink stones, and placed one at her head, and one at her feet, and some of the women planted pink roses in between them, with some red ones for the little bird, and some white ones for the puppy. "For Rose and her little friends," they said.

And to this day, there are always roses in Ermingild.

24

THE NEXT MORNING, along all the outer walls of the Realm, the vines and ancient woody thorns that lay dead longer than anyone could remember began to get tiny shoots of bright green leaves. By the second day, they all came out in full bloom. The walls were now masses of thick, bright blossoms, rich with fragrance, and everyone marveled at their beauty and sweet scent.

The miracle of renewed life that was springing up helped to heal the hearts of the Placidéans.

New roses now bloomed on the gates. Even the old, dead ivy had sprung tiny green leaves, beginning to push out the old, weather-shaken vines that clung stubbornly, partially revealing the long-hidden words in ancient script on the gates.

And Safeerah was content … the people had remembered … and her roots went back into the Realm.

On that same morning, a young couple, Galen and his wife, Yasmin, approached the gates of the Realm with their little daughter, Fenna, carefully arrayed in a new purple flowered dress her aunt had made for her. She had matching ribbons carefully attached in her tiny wisps of hair. They lived in Neesa, so they didn't have the long journey for her to enter, common for so many.

"Everything will be safe inside the Realm, I'm sure of it," Galen assured Yasmin. "Hopefully, all the sad things that have been happening are in the past now. Let's just make sure we've thought of everything our Fenna needs to be ready to enter the Realm today so she can get her Guardian. And most of all, we don't want her to be unhappy when we part at the gates."

Yasmin nodded. "I know, and she's ready," she replied simply. She and Galen briefly squeezed each other's hands for quick reassurance as they arrived at the gates and began to finish getting Fenna ready.

Yasmin hung Fenna's ceremonial bag containing the customary grain and bread offerings over her shoulder, giving her a quick hug, while Galen rang the small bell. Fenna seemed cheerful and well prepared as the gates opened.

"Mama and Papa will be here waiting for you," said her mother, kissing her on the forehead. Fenna slipped out of her mother's arms and walked confidently inside the gates.

"Blow me a hummingbird kiss!" called Galen, as he and Yasmin both blew kisses toward Fenna through the gates.

Fenna walked past the opening to the other side before turning back to wave goodbye, blowing little kisses with both her pudgy hands. "Bye-bye, Mama! Bye-bye, Papa! Birdy kisses, Papa!"

Several monks in their usual pale, ivory robes and sage colored sashes gently called out to Fenna, "Come! Come little one! Welcome to the Realm!

Come say hello to our friends!"

The monks held out their hands, and Fenna cheerfully approached them, putting one of her little hands into one of theirs, and glancing back for one last wave good-bye. The red tapestry bell pull was taken inside, and the gates closed carefully behind her.

Fenna's eyes immediately grew big with happiness. "It's a wow-wow!" she called out excitedly when she saw a little pug dog trotting towards her. He joyfully wagged his tail to greet her, skittering his dancing feet in greetings as she started to pet him. He was followed by a goose, several ducks, and a fluffy brown hen.

An older monk knelt down to her level to greet her. Two young, smiling monks stood next to him. "My name is Silas," he began. Then petting the little dog, he said, "Let me introduce you to your first friend. His name is Wags." Pointing to the two youthful Keepers who were still standing, he continued, "And these are two of my friends, Taavi and Rose."

The two Keepers smiled knowingly at each other.

As they waited for old Silas to let Fenna spend a few minutes getting to know Wags, Taavi found a pink rosebud, picked it, and playfully placed it in Rose's long golden curls. Holding hands, they turned, waiting in anticipation as they looked towards the direction of the lake. Taavi whistled, then called, "Here, boy!"

Silas glanced up curiously. As if he had been waiting for Taavi's signal, a large, white Great Pyrenees came bounding up the hill from the lake at full speed to greet everyone. He came to a running stop in front of Silas, furiously wagging his tail, curving his entire body in pure happiness, trying to climb into Silas's arms. Silas first froze in disbelief, then recognizing the huge dog, swept him up and embraced him closely, unable to hide his tears of surprise as the dog whined and barked with joy.

Taavi and Rose looked on in delight. Then they quietly took Fenna and Wags and the rest of their animal friends down the path to the lake.

Silas now sat on the ground with the joyful dog, petting him and speaking softly, his voice choked with emotion. He held the dog's head in his hands and looked straight into his eyes while the dog wrapped his paw around him.

"Good boy, my Zeke, good boy! You did it, you came back! I love you, Zeke! I love you!"

This was the Realm.